DEN OF DANGER

"Will the sound of guns carry from here to the house?" Silver asked.

"Not the noise of revolvers," said Taxi. "Not with the wind hanging where it is."

Silver looked carefully about him. When he had finished his survey, he finally said: "Well, it seems all right to me. Taxi, turn Christian's hands loose, and give him one of the Colts."

"Why?" asked Taxi.

"Because," said Silver, "the time has come for us to fight the old fight out to a finish. Either Christian or I have come to the end of the trail."

D0684611

Books by Max Brand

Ambush at Torture Canyon
The Bandit of the Black Hills
The Bells of San Filipo
Black Jack
Blood on the Trail
The Blue Jay
The Border Kid
Danger Trail
Dead or Alive
Destry Rides Again
The False Rider
Fightin' Fool
Fightin' Four
Flaming Irons
Ghost Rider (Original title: Clung)
The Gun Tamer
Gunman's Reckoning
Harrigan
Hired Guns
Hunted Riders
The Jackson Trail
Larromee's Ranch
The Longhorn Feud
The Longhorn's Ranch
The Long, Long Trail
The Man from Mustang
On the Trail of Four

The Outlaw of Buffalo Flat
The Phantom Spy
Pillar Mountain
Pleasant Jim
The Reward
Ride the Wild Trail
Riders of the Plains
Rippon Rides Double
Rustlers of Beacon Creek
The Seven of Diamonds
Seven Trails
Shotgun Law
Silvertip's Search
Silvertip's Trap
Singing Guns
Steve Train's Ordeal
The Stingaree
The Stolen Stallion
The Streak
The Tenderfoot
Thunder Moon
Tragedy Trail
Trouble Kid
The Untamed
Valley of the Vanishing Men
Valley of Thieves
Vengeance Trail

Published by POCKET BOOKS

Max Brand
VALLEY THIEVES

BOWLING GREEN STATE UNIVERSITY DISCARDED LIBRARY

PUBLISHED BY POCKET BOOKS NEW YORK

POCKET BOOKS, a Simon & Schuster division of
GULF & WESTERN CORPORATION
1230 Avenue of the Americas, New York, N.Y. 10020

Copyright 1933 by Frederick Faust; copyright renewed © 1961
by Jane F. Easton, Judith Faust and John Frederick Faust

Published by arrangement with Dodd, Mead & Company

All rights reserved, including the right to reproduce
this book or portions thereof in any form whatsoever.
For information address Dodd, Mead & Company,
79 Madison Avenue, New York, N.Y. 10016

ISBN: 0-671-83031-7

First Pocket Books printing February, 1950

10   9   8   7   6   5

Trademarks registered in the United States and other countries.

Printed in the U.S.A.

Contents

1 THE WHIRLWIND .... · 7
2 THE WHEEL 12
3 THE SIGN OF TROUBLE 18
4 THE FAMOUS MAN 24
5 CLONMEL'S AGREEMENT 29
6 AT THE CARY PLACE 35
7 SILVER'S FRIEND 40
8 TAXI'S ARRANGEMENTS 45
9 THE CARY DOMAIN 51
10 THE HEAD OF THE CLAN 55
11 WORSE TROUBLE 62
12 BARRY CHRISTIAN 67
13 ANOTHER PRISONER 73
14 THE MAN OF ACTION 78
15 GUNS IN THE DARK 84
16 THE PURSUIT 89
17 CARY'S OFFER 95
18 A CHANCE 100
19 THE SECOND ATTEMPT 106
20 A QUARREL 110
21 THE REVELATION 116
22 DEN OF DANGER 121

23 CHRISTIAN'S IDEA 129
24 END OF THE TRAIL 132
25 A NIGHT TRIP 136
26 AT BLUE WATER 141

1 / The Whirlwind

PEOPLE WHO KNOW what I've been through generally look at me twice, because, after they hear the name of Bill Avon, they have to squint at me to make sure that they are seeing right, and that I can possibly be the man who once stood in front of the evil white face of Barry Christian and lived to talk about it afterwards. All that my friends know is that I'm big enough to be awkward, big enough to make an easy target, and by no means adroit with any tool except an ax or a pitchfork. They know that I have a bit of a ranch up in the Blue Waters, where my wife and I are making a home out of acres which are green for one month of the year, brown for five, and all the rest of the time are half wind and half snow; and when they see our shack that leans against a big boulder for shelter from the north storms, they can't believe that out of that shanty came the man who knows more about Jim Silver than any other person in the world.

Well, I've been misquoted a good deal, and a lot that has been said about Jim Silver, a lot of crazy exaggeration, has been traced to me. I deny it all. I never said that Jim Silver could knock a silver dollar out of the air as far away as he could see it spin. I never said that he was never thrown by any horse. I never said that he was as good with the left hand as with the right. I never said that his horse, Parade, understood every word and sign that the master uttered. I never said that Frosty, his wolf, could read the mind of any man. What I have said is—

But I am going to put down everything as I actually know it, parting the foolish lies from the honest facts. When you get through with the account, you'll find the knowing of them has plastered ten more years of gray in my hair. I look fifty now, but I'm only a little over forty, and Christian and Silver and "Taxi" and the rest of them did that to me. Just knowing them did it to me.

First of all, it's important to explain how I happened to be caught up by the whirlwind, and how that storm carried me into the dangerous society of Jim Silver, and that soft-footed, swift-handed devil of a Taxi, and Barry Christian. Still, when I think of them, it's as though I were a child reading a book of wonders, stepping short behind seven-league boots. But as for the whirlwind itself, that picked me up and swept me along, the name of it was Harry Clonmel.

The first time I saw him was in Belling Lake. I'd gone down to the town to do the shopping for the month. My wife usually came with me; sometimes my boy was along; but Charlotte had a cold and a headache, this day, and Al stayed home to look after things. That was how I happened to be alone in Belling Lake. I had some flour and a side of bacon, a good auger for boring post holes, two hundred pounds of barbed wire, some brads, and a big new roasting pan, with odds and ends for Charlotte, all piled into the back of the buckboard. I had gone to untie the team from the hitch rack, and I was just saying a few words to "Doc" Mitchell—I remember he was pulling at one side of his long mustache and laughing at something I had just said—when I first saw Harry Clonmel.

He had the right sort of an entrance. A fanfare of horns was in order, in the old days, when the king and hero entered, and the trumpet call that was sounded for Harry Clonmel was a sudden burst of whooping and yelling down in Jack Parker's saloon.

The noise went right up to a crescendo, then guns boomed, and someone screeched. It was like the beat of a great bell just over my head, that climax to the uproar. It exploded in my brain and sent a shudder through my breastbone.

The double doors of Jack Parker's place split open like a shingle under a hatchet stroke. Instead of the blade of a hatchet, the body of a man appeared, that big, tough fellow, "Bud" Lawson. He shot out, head first, with a gun still exploding in one hand and the other arm making swimming movements in the thin of the air. He landed on his face, in the street. The deep dust spilled out from the impact, like water into spray; a cloud of white burst up; out of the cloud appeared big Bud Lawson, running.

He was not charging back toward the saloon, either. No, sir, he was sprinting the other way, and he legged it so fast that the dust was sucked a little distance after him; the wind of his speed jerked the hat off his head and blew up his long hair on end. The weight of the gun impeded him. He shied that gun away, and lifted his knees higher and higher. He was going so lickety-split that, when he reached the first corner, he had to slant himself forty-five degrees to get around the angle, out of sight.

I wondered what group of men had been enough angered by some of Lawson's tricks to grab him and throw him out of the saloon door that way. I wondered how they could be so rash, knowing that Lawson would surely hunt them down, one by one, afterwards. Out of the saloon boiled a dozen men, shouting, laughing. I knew a good many of them. They must have been drunk, to pick on Lawson, I thought.

Then I saw what had actually chucked Lawson into the air like a sawdust doll. It was a dark-haired fellow who came half-way out the saloon entrance and paused there, resting his hand on top of the door.

Resting his hand *on top* of the door, I said, and meant it. Why, he was a regular whale, that fellow. I never knew his feet and inches. Six four, six five—I don't know what he was. Nobody ever wanted to put a measuring rod on him or ask a scales how many pounds he weighed. All the mind said when it looked at him was: "He's big enough!" He overflowed the imagination. The idea of him ran out onto the margin of the page, so to speak. Because, no matter how big his body was, the spirit in him was bigger still. I could see the gloss and sheen of his dark hair; I could see the dark gloss and the fire of his eyes even at that distance, and the laughter that was bursting from his lips rang in my head as though some huge, bell-mouthed trumpet had been placed at my ear, and blown.

When he stopped laughing, there was still a tremor in

9

me, as though a quiver had come out of the ground and remained in the weak of my knees.

He stepped back inside the door, and the rest of the crowd—like silly little children dressed up in long pants—followed after that real man.

Doc Mitchell was a hardy fellow, with the sort of a vocabulary that is picked up while freighting with mule teams across the mountain desert, but even he could find nothing to say now, though he seemed to be trying.

I looked at Doc and wanted to laugh, but there wasn't any laughter in me. I had been emptied of everything, including speech.

After a while, Doc said: "Big wind, don't you blow my way!" He began to laugh helplessly, his eyes going in a foolish way from side to side. I began to laugh, too, and knew the same idiocy was in my face.

"There's a whole lot of business in that hombre," I said.

"There's a whole month of Sunday meetings in him," said Doc Mitchell.

"Lawson is no fool," I said.

"He's a real bright boy," said Doc Mitchell. "He knows when to pick his feet up fast and put them down far apart."

Sheriff Walt Milton slanted around the next corner on a cayuse and came along ding-bust-it for the two of us. He pulled up his nag. The spade of his Spanish bit pried the mouth of his bronco wide open; I saw the bloody froth drooling, and the fear and agony like blood in the eyes of the horse, too.

Walt was the sort of a fellow who was always in a hurry, and he always seemed to have his teeth set just right for a fight. He was a sandy man, both ways you take the word. There was no yellow in him, and, also, his complexion and hair were so faded that there appeared to be dust in his eyebrows, and dust seemed to be always in the wrinkles of his face. Even his eyes were a sort of straw color. The brighter they got, the paler they grew. He was a man-killer, was Walt Milton. We all knew that; we all were sure that he liked his job, not for the salary, but for the shooting chances that went with it. But we kept on voting for him because a mild sheriff would have been no good with the wild fellows in our neck of the woods.

I talk about Walt Milton because he had a big hand in what was to come. He sang out, as he pulled up his horse:

"What's this I hear about a shooting scrape in Parker's place?"

"A big hombre in there just threw Bud Lawson out on his head," I told Milton. "Lawson seemed to be doing the shooting, and the stranger was using his hands."

"Just his hands?" said Milton, with half of a smile.

He rode on to Parker's place, got off, and went inside. Whatever he saw and heard in there seemed to satisfy him. He came out, got on his horse, and jogged slowly past us down the street, with a thoughtful look on his face.

Doc Mitchell muttered: "Walt is tasting a big fight with that big stranger. It oughta be something worth while."

I started to untie my team again, but out of Parker's saloon appeared the big young man once more, with the crowd following, stretching their legs to keep up with him. The nearer he came striding toward us, the bigger he loomed, but he carried his weight like a racer. He was put together with springs.

I could see why Bud Lawson had picked on him. It was because there was such bright good nature in his face. There was a spring of it in his heart, and it kept overflowing at his eyes.

He went on up the street and turned in at Denny McRae's place. I retied the lead rope I had unknotted and looked at Doc Mitchell, and Doc looked at me. Then, without a word, we tagged along to see the fun.

2 / The Wheel

HARRY CLONMEL—we all learned his name shortly after we got into McRae's place—was flush and treating the crowd. He laid down his money as though it were dirt, while my worried mind kept translating those dollars into bacon, blankets, and beef on the hoof. You could see that money was not what Clonmel wanted to take from the world. He set up a couple of rounds and then drifted back into the long, narrow game room at the back of the saloon. In five minutes he had the games going, and McRae appeared from nowhere, going about in his usual down-headed way, looking up with his suspicious and sullen glances.

"Somebody ought to tell Clonmel that McRae's the brother-in-law of the sheriff," said Doc Mitchell to me.

"What good would that do?" I asked Doc. "You wouldn't show cake to a baby, so why now show trouble to Clonmel?"

Mitchell chuckled at that. But I've regretted since that day that one of us didn't give Harry Clonmel some good advice before the crash came. However, there was not a word said, and in a little while, Clonmel was bucking roulette and making a big play. He sluiced out the money with both hands, won a thousand, lost a thousand, kept right on losing.

"I wonder if that's honest money?" I said to Mitchell. "It doesn't seem to have any weight with Clonmel!"

He'd struck a bad losing streak, as a matter of fact. McRae had sent his regular dealer and croupier off the job and was spinning the wheel himself, seeming to despise the coin he was taking in. But I saw his nostrils begin to flare. As a matter of fact, I think that Clonmel pushed five or six thousand dollars into that machine be-

12

fore he stopped, all at once, rubbed his knuckles across his chin, and laid a sudden hold on the machine.

It was bolted into the floor, of course, but that didn't hold it now. The pedestal tilted. The bolts came ripping and groaning out of the wood.

I looked at McRae and saw him snap out a gun. Well, I had been expecting that, and I just grabbed his gun wrist and said:

"He'll pay for the damage, Denny."

"Blast you!" said McRae to me, but he didn't try to free himself.

The roulette outfit went over with a crash; the cowpunchers cracked the roof open with their yells. And then I heard Harry Clonmel lift his voice. The boom and the ring of it lodged somewhere in my mind so deeply that I can still hear the roar.

"Crooked as hell!" he shouted. "There's the brake McRae's been using!"

We could all see it, fitted under the floor boards, with the pin for his foot's pressure sticking up a trifle through a crack. A light touch on that lever would put the necessary drag on the wheel at the right instant, as the whirling died away to slowness. The weight of a breath could control the roulette wheel at that stage.

I couldn't believe what I saw. I had never liked McRae. Nobody ever had. But it wasn't possible, you'd say, for a fellow to be raised in a town from his boyhood and then install crooked machinery to make sure of stealing the money of his friends. Stealing? Why, a thief is an honest man, a hero, and a gentleman, compared with a dirty snake who cheats at a game of chance.

The impossibility of what I was seeing there under the broken flooring turned me numb and dumb. It froze up the rest of the men, and that gace McRae a chance to be a murderer as well as a sneak. He got his hand away from my grip, pulled up the nose of his Colt, and fired pointblank.

He could not miss, you'd say. Not a target as high and as wide as Harry Clonmel. Besides, McRae was known as a fighting man. It was said that the only reason the sheriff let McRae marry his sister was that he was afraid of having trouble with Denny. And we all knew that McRae spend a couple of hours every day practicing to keep his hand in.

Yet Denny missed on this occasion, because as he pulled his hand free and moved his Colt, Harry Clonmel got in motion, too. He took a step forward and hit McRae with the full sweep of his left arm. McRae's bullet drove under the shoulder of Clonmel, knocked a pipe out of the teeth of Pete Meany, and went slam into a big joist at the end of the room. McRae himself was lifted off his feet at the same instant by Clonmel's punch. There must have been lift as well as drive in that wallop, because McRae trailed in the air, turned in it, and landed with a whang, on his face.

Clonmel turned aside and emptied the cash drawer of the roulette outfit into his pockets. He was entirely calm. Excitement makes a man puff more than mountain climbing, but Clonmel was not breathing hard. He counted out the sum of money that he had lost, and since there was plenty more than that left, he pushed it over, and the crowd helped itself.

No one went near McRae, who began to lift himself from the floor. His face was a red blur. The punch had smashed his nose flat. His eyes were beginning to swell already, and the blood ran out of him in an amazing way. He looked as though he'd been slammed in the face by a fourteen-pound sledge, or the steel knuckle of a great walking beam. A trickle of red was even running out of his ears. It was a miracle that he could recover consciousness so soon.

However, he soon was on his knees, then on his feet, swaying, when his reserves opened a back door and came on the charge into the room. The bartender was one of them; two more were bouncers; they were all good fighting men, when it came to gun work, and I expected to see Clonmel go down full of lead.

Everyone else expected gunfire, too, and the boys dived for doors and threw themselves under tables. But not a single weapon exploded. Harry Clonmel was the reason. He had picked up McRae by the neck and the belt, and now he heaved the gambler right at the three fighting men. They went down with a crash.

When they got up, they were headed in the opposite direction. They made tracks out of that room pronto.

I wanted to laugh, but I knew that it was no laughing matter. McRae was out of the picture, but not for long. He'd try to kill Clonmel. He *had* to kill Clonmel. If he were hanged for the murder, later on, that couldn't mean much more than what had already happened to him. He was a ruined man. The only thing he knew how to do was to run a saloon, and now the fame of his crookedness would travel all over the West. McRae might as well go out and howl with the wolves, and before he did that he would certainly try to get even with the giant.

Then there was the sheriff.

Well, the rest of the boys seemed to figure things the same way. They eased out of McRae's place as fast as they could go. Only Clonmel was in no hurry. He sat down, made a cigarette, and lighted it. I was amazed at him.

"Clonmel," I said, "do you have to stay here like this?"

He looked over at me and nodded.

"They may want to come back and talk," he said, "and I ought to be here to listen."

"Do you as much as carry a gun?" I asked him.

"No," said he.

It was the answer I expected, but it staggered me just the same.

"You've showed a lot of nerve and a strong hand, but you've had some luck, too," I said to him. "Now you go saddle your horse and get out of this town, because when McRae comes back, he'll have the sheriff with him!"

"The sheriff?" asked Clonmel. "Does he herd with crooked gamblers in this town?"

"The sheriff's the brother-in-law of McRae," I answered him, "and he doesn't know how to miss with a gun. And he's coming here to collect your scalp. Do you understand?"

He nodded. After what he had done, you would expect to see a bit of the savage in his face, but, on the contrary, there was no sign of that. Instead, he was simply shining with good nature and high color, like a small boy who has just finished a good round of tag. There

15

was a blur of red on the knuckles of his left hand; that was the only mark that appeared on him. I could not help wondering what would have happened to the face of the gambler if Clonmel had hit him with his right. Now he sat back in his chair and continued to smile at me, though the sheen of his eyes had diminished a little.

"I understand that the sheriff is coming for me," he said. "I've never run away from a sheriff before and I don't want to begin doing it now. I'll stay here and wait."

I got so excited that I went up and grabbed him by the arm. It was like laying hold of the leg of a horse. I shook the heavy, loose weight of the arm and shouted:

"Clonmel, you don't know the sheriff. He's a killer. He'll kill you! Clonmel, do you hear me? Can you use a gun?"

"I can hit things with a rifle, now and then," said Clonmel. "I never used a revolver in my life."

"You'll be murdered!" I cried at him. "You fool, I know what I'm saying."

Clonmel took hold of my hands gently and moved me a little away from him.

"You want to help me," he admitted, "but it's not any use, and I don't want you to get into trouble. If the sheriff wants to see me—well, I'll have to stay here till he arrives."

It was like arguing with a woman, adding up two and two and two, and finding that they make zero. Then, before I could say a word more, a door opened, and the sheriff stood there. He wasn't raging. He was all cold, and there was a stony smile chiseled out around his mouth.

"Clonmel," he said, "you're a bully and a big-mouthed cur. I've come to get you—in the name of the law!"

When he mentioned the law, his grin turned from stone to iron and froze wider on his face. Law? Well, it was gun law that he meant.

Clonmel swayed forward to rise. Then I shouted:

"Sit still! If you get on your feet, he'll murder you. Sheriff, this is an unarmed man!"

"You lie," said the sheriff. "The yellow dog is going to get up and fill his hand."

16

I got so angry that I forgot to be afraid. I jumped in between them and shook my finger at the sheriff.

Behind me I could feel Clonmel rising like a mighty shadow.

"If you pull a gun on him," I yelled at the sheriff, "I'll have a lynching posse after you. I'll bring this up to the law courts. I'll tell 'em what I know—that Clonmel hasn't a gun! Milton, keep your hand away from that Colt!"

The sheriff managed to center some attention on me, when he heard this. He had worked himself right up to the killing point. Now he saw that raw meat was being snatched away from his teeth and he shuddered like a crazy bull terrier.

But the truth of what I had said struck him harder than bullets. I wasn't a drinking man; I wasn't a fighting man; I was, in fact, just a dull, ordinary drone of a worker, trying to make a home and paying my debts as they came up. For that reason, in a law court my testimony would be about ten times as heavy as all the thugs and crooks and hangers-on of the gambling dump put together. Besides, in a society of cowpunchers and young miners and prospectors, I was a fairly old man. All of these things began to add up in the mind of the sheriff. I could see them clicking in his eyes as big Clonmel pushed me gently to the side. The sweep of his arm was like the drive of a downstream current.

"I don't need anyone between you and me," said Clonmel to the sheriff. "You've used some language that—"

"Oh, hell," said Walt Milton, and turned on his heel and walked away.

Clonmel started after him. I ran in front of him and held out my hands. He walked into them. My arms buckled under the weight of him.

"Are you going to be fool enough to play his game?" I asked.

His lips worked a couple of times before he managed to unlock his jaws and answer:

"You're right. I've got to—I've got to learn how to shoot if I stay in this part of the country. If—"

He shut his teeth on the rest of it. Learn to shoot? Why,

17

those hands on his were too big to be very fast, and what could he learn compared with the gun knowledge of men who were born with the smell of gunpowder in the air? He could only learn enough to make one first gesture, which would be his last. I could see the bullets smashing into his body, into his handsome face. It turned me sick.

"Clonmel," I said, "come up to my ranch and go to work for me. I'll teach you to shoot on the side."

It was the vaguest sort of a gesture on my part. I thought at first that he didn't hear me, because he was still staring through the doorway after Walt Milton. I was a good deal surprised when he pried his jaws open to answer:

"Thanks. I'll do it."

3 / The Sign of Trouble

WHEN I GOT Harry Clonmel up to the ranch, I felt somewhat as though I'd landed a fighting pike in a small boat. There was going to be trouble ahead. How much trouble, I couldn't guess, but I imagined that one face of it would be Sheriff Walt Milton.

If only he had been the worst of it! But, of course, back there in the beginning of things, I couldn't dream what was going to happen. I simply knew that Clonmel was an explosive and that, when he burst, a good many things might be broken. But, like an old sea story, everything went well at first, and we had nothing but clear skies and cheerful days.

Clonmel liked the life up there in the Blue Water Mountains. He liked the air and the beauty of the big peaks. He liked my wife, and my wife liked him. Charlotte was a big, soft, pretty girl when I married her. She kept on getting bigger and softer, but she lost her prettiness. She used to rub her face with cold cream, a good deal, and she'd lie in bed late on Sunday morning to rest her features, but the pink and the smile of her prettiness would never come back. She was a good, cheerful, hearty woman, in lots of ways, but she had a pride of her own. She spoke careful English, smiled at the lingo of the cowpunchers, and raised our boy with an idea in the back of his head that somehow he came of better blood than most. Such ideas are dangerous, of course, but Charlotte had to have something to keep her head in the air.

She said that Harry Clonmel was a gentleman and that he would be a good influence for our boy, Al. As a matter of fact, it was Al who seemed to be top dog of the two, most of the time. Al was twelve, tough as hickory, and knew all about range ways and mountain life. It was Al who became special instructor of Clonmel in using a rope, in riding broncos, in shooting with a rifle or with a revolver. They spent every spare moment that he had on those jobs.

But all during the working hours of the day, Clonmel kept with me. I never saw a better worker, because he was the strongest man I've ever found, and in addition to that he had a fire of vast cheerfulness always stoked up and burning bright inside him. A cheerful man doesn't get tired easily; a cheerful man keeps his eyes open and knows what's happening around him. I never had to tell Clonmel things twice. He used his brains as much as he used his big hands.

And what hands—and what they could do! The meanest job on a ranch is building fence, but Clonmel could eat a hole in hard ground in no time, with a boring auger, and he would carry about an armful of the heavy posts as though they were fagots for the kitchen stove. There wasn't much need of a lever to pull the wire lines tight. A heave of his big shoulders was generally enough to draw the heavy barbed wire until it shuddered. Of course, there were a lot of things that Clonmel knew nothing about, but though he might start a day helplessly, he generally had done more work, by evening, then three ordinary hands, no matter how experienced they happened to be.

Nothing made him sick, either. He could shrug away weariness with one gesture of his shoulders, and at the end of a day he would wash, comb his hair, and sit down at our table, shining with good nature. I can tell you that we lived well while he was with us, because my wife worked overtime to please the taste and fill the huge maw of Harry. Her trouble was always repaid, because he could eat for five as easily as he could work for ten. He was a good talker, too, and he kept us laughing with his chatter when he sat about in the evening. There was only one thing that shut him up, and that was to ask him why he was in the West.

He dodged that question; all we could make out was that he was hunting for something or someone. He never would tell us precisely what he wanted, but we got the idea that in our country, somewhere, he expected to find what he was looking for, and that, in the meantime, he was glad to grow accustomed to Western ways and harden himself in the new life. Whatever it was that he had before him, he apparently expected that it might take him a great part of his life.

Charlotte and I used to put our heads together and conjecture. I had an idea that he might have done something that forced him out of his home to save his neck. If he lost his temper in a fight, for instance, he might easily have killed a man. But Charlotte declared that no man outside the law could have an eye so open, so clear, and so bright.

Well, those were good days, take them all in all. Al and Harry slept up in the attic, and when Charlotte's alarm clock rattled the call for the day's work to begin, we'd hear the tremendous bellow of Harry in answer, like the booming of a bull moose.

Yes, those were good days, but they couldn't last long, and the first sign of the trouble to come was the appearance of a woman. Julie Perigord walked in on us, one afternoon, and knocked the spots out of our peaceful existence.

It happened like this:

The day had been hot and close, but in the middle of the afternoon the wind changed, a cloud showed its black shoulders in the northwest behind Mount Craven, and in twenty minutes the storm was screaming, and the cattle

20

were drifting at a trot, lowering their heads away from the wind.

The sky blackened over. The chill blew through our bones. Winter came back in the middle of summer and darkened the world for us. I got hold of Harry Clonmel and took him back to the house with me.

He merely said: "This is all right. This is what a fellow sees from the lowlands, when the clouds come—zoom! Right across the heads of the mountains. I've always wanted to be inside the clouds, one day."

"You and the lightning, eh?" said I, and right on the heels of my words, the lightning started dancing in the rain like a hundred red devils.

We got back to the house, and Charlotte made us some coffee. We sat in the kitchen, as usual, and watched Charlotte mix up the batter for a cake. She'd started baking a cake a lot after Harry came out to us.

It was warm and pleasant, sitting in there with the storm yelling louder all the while, drawing back, and then charging us, and laying hands on the shack until the pans started shivering and rattling against one another along the kitchen wall. I remember saying that we would have to dig the foundations and get ready to build another place—not of boards, but of logs. Harry and I would start felling the trees right away.

"Dad," Al said, "you always talk about building a house, but we're never going to have a good one."

"Why not?" I asked him.

"Because Ma wants a cave or a palace; she don't want nothing in between," said Al.

I looked down at the floor to cover my grin, because what Al said of Charlotte was just about true. She remarked:

"I don't want you to refer to me as 'Ma,' and how does 'don't want nothing' sound to your own ears, Alfred?"

"Is it wrong?" asked Al.

She was so angry at that, that she began to breathe fast and hard.

"You know perfectly well it's wrong," she said. "If it's the last act of my life, I'm going to insist on good grammar from you, Alfred. It takes just as much breath to speak incorrectly as it does to use proper words."

"I heard old Pie Jennings talk the other day," said Al. "He don't have to stop when he draws in his breath. It's like whistling, the way he talks. He was swearing at his off leader, and the way he burned that gray mule was enough to—"

"Oh, Bill Avon," said Charlotte to me, "do you see what's happening to my son? Do you see how rude, rough, vulgar men are going to—"

She came to a stop, her voice all trembling.

I was uncomfortable. Al looked at Harry Clonmel, and Clonmel looked back at Al with an empty eye. Just then the wind whistled on its highest pitch, a blow fell against the kitchen door, it was jerked open, and Julie Perigord came into the room with a sway and a stagger. The draft went rattling off through the house as Clonmel reached the door and shoved it shut.

"Wow!" said Julie. "What a zipper this one is!"

She was very cold. The white of it had fingered her face, here and there, and the blue shadow was around her mouth.

I asked her where her horse was; she said that she'd put it up herself before she came into the house. That touched me. She was such a headlong, wild girl, that one didn't expect her to show so much consideration.

Charlotte pulled off the dripping slicker and wrapped Julie in a big blanket. It made her look like an Indian, what with her black hair and brown-black eyes and her swarthy skin—before the color came up in her cheeks.

"What brought you up here in this sort of weather?" asked Charlotte. "The storm must have been in sight for some time before you ever started through the pass."

"Of course it was," said Julie. "But Will Cary told me not to start and he was so proud and strong and sure of everything that I just came along anyway, to put him in his place." She explained to Harry Clonmel: "Will Cary's the fellow who's going to marry me. That's what he says, anyway."

Clonmel said nothing. He just got hold of the coffee pot and poured her a cup of the coffee. The he stood by and

22

watched her sipping the hot stuff, and his eyes kept drifting contentedly from the cup to her face and back again. It was easy to see that he could keep on looking for a long time. That was no wonder. Julie was the sort of a girl who knocks the spots out of a crowd of other girls as soon as she appears. She trailed a dust cloud over all the other females every time she rode by. The brightness of her seemed to put Charlotte, for instance, right out of the room.

I remember thinking, as I looked at her, that it would take somebody like Will Cary to rouse her even to disobedience. She had the daring of any man, the strength of most men, and a spirit, in addition, that could have been the admiration of arch fiend or archangel. Clonmel was feeding his eyes on her. I knew, somehow, that the results of this day would be more than apparent later on.

The first effects were not long in showing.

Charlotte was saying: "You know, Julie, that you can't trifle with Will Cary."

"Will can't trifle with me," said Julie. "He has to know that, too. I'm not the sort to marry a man and leave him."

That was rather neatly put. She would do her finding out before she took the step that might be irrevocable in her eyes. It was always that way with Julie. She might do a great deal of balking and shying, but always because she thought she saw something wrong.

"Commands are a temptation—to some people," I said. "Will ought to know by this time."

She paid no attention to me, for a moment. She had found Harry Clonmel with her mind as well as with her eyes, and she was staring at him with a frank interest, half smiling with pleasure to see such a sight.

"That's a lot of man to find inside of one skin," she said. "Why don't you introduce me, Bill?"

4 / The Famous Man

WHEN I INTRODUCED THEM, they each wore a faint smile, faintly shining eyes, as though each understood that a good deal was being seen at that moment.

"You've tucked yourself into a quiet corner," said Julie. "Who are you going to scare when you pop out?"

He kept on smiling at her, as though answering with words would be no good at all. But Al piped up:

"He's the strongest man you ever saw, Julie."

"Well, I've seen some strong ones," said Julie. "That's why riding through the pass into the storm was worth while. You know who I saw in the narrows of the pass, Charlotte?"

My wife gaped and waited.

"I saw the last man in the world that you'd expect. I saw Jim Silver," said Julie.

That famous name came home to me with a shock. It always did. I never had seen him, but he had been in the Blue Waters almost more than in any other part of the West, and, of course, I had heard plenty of stories about him. Charlotte had actually met him, and she told us how gentle and kind he was.

"You saw Jim Silver?" she cried now.

"I did. I was Jim Silver, and Parade, and Frosty, too. That's the biggest dog I ever saw, Charlotte. He's a whale. If he isn't a wolf, he's first cousin of a wolf."

"Frosty *is* a wolf," said I.

"Nonsense," said my wife. "No wolf was ever tamed."

"This one is only tame for Silver," said I.

"Don't split hairs," said Charlotte testily. "Go on, Julie. You saw Jim Silver? My goodness, when I saw him— But you'd seen him before?"

"I hadn't. Not with my own eyes. I've heard so much about him, though, that I should have recognized him.

24

But it was only Parade and Frosty that spotted him for me. That stallion is big enough to carry even you, Harry Clonmel, as easily as a feather."

"Maybe I'd better get that horse, then," said Clonmel.

The girl laughed. So did Charlotte and I. Other men had tried to get the big golden stallion from Jim Silver. What happened to them was enough to fill a book.

"When you get Parade, get Frosty, too," said Julie Perigord. "Silver has made a team of them. You might as well do the same thing."

"Why not?" said Clonmel.

"Well, when you get 'em, come ask me to go riding with you, will you?" said Julie. She went on to say to my wife: "I could see Parade shine through the clouds! The fog was blowing through the pass, and I saw Parade shine as though he were a horse of gold. And then I spotted Frosty, running back like a wisp of the gray mist to report to his master, I suppose. Afterward, I lost sight of them. The mist was closing in. When it cleared again, close by me, Jim Silver came breaking out of the cloud, with Frosty showing the way and snarling up at me. I mean, Frosty was doing the snarling."

She laughed in her excitement.

Then she went on: "He looked younger than I had expected. I don't think that he's more than thirty. He came right up to me and lifted his hat, and I saw the tufts of gray hair over his temples, like the beginning of little horns. He's handsome. I never knew that. Very brown and handsome, and he has a smile that warms the heart. He told me that I should know that it's dangerous to be up in the pass when the wind blows out of the northwest. I told him that I was all right. He said that I ought to let him come along with me until I was in a safe place. And I wanted to have him come, too, but all at once I thought what a little coward and worthless fool I was, if I took Jim Silver off his trail.

"He was probably hunting Barry Christian again, for all that I knew. I couldn't turn him aside. I swore that I was all right. He told me if I grew confused and couldn't find shelter, if the storm grew any worse, I was to keep on up the mountain along the side of the creek, and I'd find his camp. He'd take care of me. That was romantic enough. Think of sitting at Jim Silver's campfire and having him tell stories to you—about Parade and Frosty, and the trail of Barry Christian. Do you think, Bill, that Barry Christian can be in this part of the world now, since his jail break? Is that why Jim Silver has appeared?"

I shrugged my shoulders and said what everyone knows —that Jim Silver has other reasons for his strange migrations than the trail of Barry Christian. As well ask a swallow why it flies south for the winter and north for the summer as to ask why Jim Silver appeared and disappeared.

"I've heard of Jim Silver," said Clonmel. "He's a lot of man, I've heard."

"Have you *really* heard of Jim Silver?" said Julie Perigord, mockingly. "You're a real Westerner then, Harry. You must live right on their earth with the rest of us. He's even heard of Jim Silver, Charlotte," she ran on. "Isn't that wonderful? He can probably fry bacon and eat eggs, too. He's not a tenderfoot, after all."

Clonmel smiled right through this bantering, but he was not very amused by it. His color grew a little warmer.

The wind had stopped screaming so loudly by this time. The girl said that she ought to think of starting back, and Clonmel suggested that he should go with her.

"And take me home—where Will Cary could see you?" asked Julie, who was a little too frank at all times. "You may be so hardy that you've heard of Jim Silver, but I wouldn't have you meet Will Cary at the end of a trail. No, I'll be able to take care of myself."

It was a cruel speech. I blushed for Julie. I blushed for poor Harry Clonmel because he had to listen to it. I saw his jaw set and knew that he meant to make trouble, because of this.

But what trouble could he make? He was a fighting man, a fearless man, but he simply was not familiar with the language of knives and guns that savages like Will Cary spoke. And why ask a man to go to Mars unless he knows the language of the Martians, or can stay long enough to learn it? My big friend Clonmel had done very well, indeed. He was almost at the level of my son Al,

26

with a rifle, and already he was better than Al when it came to handling a man-sized .45 Colt. But that meant that, in mountain parlance, he had exactly a small boy's chance against such warriors as Will Cary. The brutal unfairness of the system against which Clonmel had to compete, struck me hard, just then.

The wind started whistling again.

"If you don't want me to take you home," said Clonmel, "perhaps I'd better go ahead and warn them that you're spending the night here?"

"Oh, they won't care where I am," said Julie. "Dean Cary would be glad to have me blown away for good and all. And if Will gives a rap—well, it will teach him not to give me orders next time. He can let me do as I please!"

There was a good deal of the savage in Julie, all right. I started to protest. Then the wind yelled louder than before. Clonmel said:

"I'd better go tell the Carys that she's staying over night. Hadn't I?"

"Nonsense!" cried Julie. "I'll ride back by myself. If *he* can ride through this weather, I can, too. I'll be my own messenger—and get laughed at for the news I bring!"

She was in a bitter, irritated humor. I suppose she saw that she had put herself in a foolish position, and it was hard for her to feel humble as a result.

There was no need for her to tag her last speech by exclaiming, finally: "A fine thing if I let a tenderfoot get frost-bitten running errands for me!"

She laughed a little as she said that. Clonmel closed his eyes. I think he wanted to break her pretty neck, just then. So did I.

"Tie up your tongue, Julie," I said. "You can see this is no laughing matter. You can't go back through this sort of weather. Listen to that wind!"

"Oh, can't I go back?" she asked dangerously.

"No. I won't let you," said I.

"Don't talk that way to me, please," said Julie, with a good deal of devil in her eyes.

She was acting like a five-year-old. She knew it, and that didn't make it any better.

27

Charlotte laughed a little and said:

"The Carys are going to be worried because you're gone, but I don't know what we can do, until the wind drops a little. Certainly you can't go back there alone."

"Oh, can't I? I'm going, though," said Julie, and stepped to the door.

I was too amazed by her to interfere. Big Clonmel made one step and caught her wrist.

"Don't be a little fool," he said.

It hit me like a fist. It seemed to hit Julie, too. She turned slowly away from the door. Her face was frozen, she was so moved. She said:

"I *have* been making a fool of myself. Excuse me, Charlotte. Someone had to tell me sooner or later, I suppose."

The wind whistled "Yes" outside the shack. Hail rattled in a volley against the walls of the house, and Charlotte tried to get the talk away to more agreeable tracks. She said that we would simply have to wait until the weather cleared a little. If it got much better, then one of the men would take Julie home—it was only an hour or so through the pass. The one who took her could stay the night at the Cary house. Otherwise, if it were possible, one of us must press through and tell the Cary family that she was safe at our house.

"I'd like to see this Jim Silver," Clonmel said. "What's the look of him?"

"He's all man," said Julie, "but he's such a gentleman that some people are fooled."

She put a lot of sting in that, avoiding the face of Clonmel with her eyes. Charlotte was the good Samaritan again and started rattling along about the time *she* had seen Jim Silver. Then she got out a picture of him and handed it to Clonmel.

I looked at it over his shoulder, because it did a man good to see even the picture of Jim Silver and to know that such a man was standing for decency and kindness and law wherever he appeared in the mountains.

Even the snapshot showed something of the kindness and steadiness and calm of that man—such a hero that

28

other men could not feel jealousy on account of his reputation.

I was thinking these things, when I touched the shoulder of Clonmel with mine, and felt a slight shudder running through him.

"I'd like to meet him," he said suddenly.

"Jim Silver?" echoed the girl.

Clonmel lifted his head, but looked at the wall, not at the girl.

"Yes," he said. "I've got to meet him."

"When you do," said the girl, "bring back a souvenir to the rest of us. Parade and Frosty, for instance."

"Would that mean something to you?" asked Clonmel through his teeth.

"I'd leave home for such a man as that," said Julie carelessly.

"We'll have to see about that," said Clonmel, and I saw, with a shock, that he was not smiling.

5 / Clonmel's Agreement

WE WOUND UP with a bad compromise. That storm kept on smashing out of the northwest, and Julie would not let one of the men take news back to the Cary house about where she was, and certainly we could not let her go back by herself. So we wound up by staying where we were. We went to bed, at last, with Al and big Clonmel in the attic, as usual, and Julie tucked away on a couch in the front room. It had been a jolly evening. We had a little second-hand organ, and my wife pumped away on it, and made it wheeze out tunes that we all sang to. It was a good thing to hear Clonmel's voice lift and boom and ring, with the soprano of Julie brightening over it like white tips over the shouldering waves. And one of the best parts of the singing was to watch the way the eyes of

Clonmel and Julie met in the middle of a passage, laughing at each other and loving the music.

When we were alone, my wife said to me: "Bill, there's going to be a lot of trouble. Harry Clonmel is out of his head about Julie, and Julie is a little bit staggered by the size and the looks of Harry Clonmel."

"No," said I. "She kept badgering him all the time, looking down on him as though she despised him a little —except when they were singing together."

"Nonsense!" said my wife. "Men have no eyes. Great, blind, hulking, blundering, thick-handed numb-wits! What can they see of the thing that are going on inside the minds of people? As plain as day, that girl was drawing on poor Harry Clonmel."

Charlotte had a way of piling up words in this manner.

I said angrily: "I don't see that Harry needs pity. They'd make a fine match."

"As well matched as two runaway horses in one team!" said Charlotte. "What are you thinking of? Do you imagine that Will Cary will let another man even look sidewise at Julie?"

That was true. I went to sleep in gloom, knowing that Harry Clonmel had put the whole of his headlong will on Julie, and that Cary was bound to make trouble. But how could such a fellow as Clonmel get through life without striking reefs? He drew too big a draft, so to speak, and small harbors would never hold him; he simply had to sail the open seas.

Well, in the morning the alarm clock sounded, and I half wakened and waited for the booming call of Clonmel in the attic, to set the house in motion. But the call did not come. Something about the silence got me out of bed and into my clothes in jig time. And when I stepped outside the house, I saw Al looking worried.

"Where's Harry?" I asked him.

"I don't know. He wasn't in the attic when the alarm went off. Maybe he's out at the barn," said Al.

But Harry was not at the barn. He was nowhere around the place, and he did not show up for breakfast, either. It was a queer, nervous sort of a breakfast, with Julie Perigord looking absently off into the distance and seeming to listen to the last uproar of the storm which had begun to clear out of the northwest so that we could see the big shoulders of Mount Craven butting through the windy mists.

Nobody talked about Harry Clonmel. He had left his pack, but he had taken his mustang. Then where could he have gone? We couldn't guess, and, therefore, we were silent.

We had finished breakfast, very nearly, when a sound of singing blew down the wind. That organ note could come out of only one throat. We glanced at one another, alarmed, pleased, conjecturing. Then we all started up and hurried out through the kitchen door.

What I saw still freezes my mind when I think of it. The pen stands still above the paper and won't write it down, for out there on his mustang, coming along at a good canter, was big Harry Clonmel, and on a lead rope beside him was Parade!

There was no doubt about it. I never had laid eyes on the famous stallion before, but the beauty and the gold of him shone in my eyes and I knew that that was Parade, at last—Jim Silver's horse on the lead rope of Clonmel!

That was enough, but it wasn't all, for beside Parade, hitched to him by another rope, heavily muzzled to keep his clever teeth harmless, skulked the biggest gray wolf that I've ever seen, a dust-colored monster of a hundred and fifty pounds, if he was an ounce.

And I knew that that was Frosty who served Jim Silver in many ways that a man could never compass, whose nose and ears and teeth and cunning were at the beck and call of his master.

There they came toward us, the stallion keeping pace with the fast canter of the mustang by gliding along at an easy trot. Up they swept; the mustang skidded to a halt, Harry Clonmel flung himself to the ground and cried out:

"You wanted to see 'em, Julie. Here they are!"

Great Scott! The words hammered against my brain. She had said, the night before, that she would leave home for the man who could take the stallion and the wolf

31

away from Jim Silver. And here Harry had accomplished the marvel.

He had paid some price for the job. There was a bandage twisted about his head with a stain of red on it, as though a bullet or a knife might have glanced as close as this to his life. But it was merely a scratch, and Clonmel was bursting with happy merriment.

Then I thought of another thing. If the stallion and the wolf were here, there could be only one explanation. Jim Silver was dead. He would certainly have fought to the end for Parade, to say nothing of Frosty, and if Jim Silver were dead, the greatest figure in the whole range of mountains had been brushed away, the greatest force for law and order had been removed from that wild land.

My wife, in a shrilling voice, cried out: "Harry, have you murdered Jim Silver?"

"Murdered him? He's as full of life as a cricket," said Harry Clonmel.

"You've killed him! You murdered him, you wretched—" began Charlotte, but the booming voice of Clonmel silenced and overrode her, saying:

"Jim Silver and I simply made a little agreement, and there's no harm done."

He began to laugh again.

Agreement? I thought to myself, what agreement would Jim Silver make to give up Parade and Frosty? What agreement would he make unless the grasp of Clonmel had first mastered to helplessness even the terrible hands of Silver?

The thing made me shudder. It was horrible. It would have been like seeing a child beat a grown man. It would be like seeing a wasp, with the hypnotic hum of his wings, freeze a spider to weakness. It would be like anything unnatural and, therefore, disgusting, if Harry Clonmel, for all his size, his power, his courage, could stand for an instant in fight before famous Jim Silver.

But there stood Clonmel, laughing, and yonder were Parade and the wolf!

Well, the world spun around before my eyes. The stallion threw up his head, turned, and sent his trumpet sound of neighing toward the mountains out of which the last shreds of the storm were blowing. He was calling his master, and the wolf sat down on his haunches and pointed his nose toward the same mountains and howled dismally.

"You wanted to see Parade and Frosty," said Clonmel to the girl. "Well, how would you like to ride Parade home?"

"Ride Parade!" she exclaimed, and her eyes shone. "Ride Parade? But only Jim Silver can ride him. He'll throw and savage any other person!"

"That's true for some," said Clonmel, "but he's no longer the same wild-caught hawk that he was when Silver trailed him down in the desert. He won't savage me, for instance."

He stepped right up to the golden stallion, and Parade, stretching his head, blew a breath from his wide red nostrils on the giant. His flattened ears twitched suddenly forward. It was plain that he looked upon this man as a friend, and my heart sickened strangely in me; it was like seeing treachery in a dumb beast.

Charlotte said: "You're not going to ride Parade, Julie. Great heavens, what are you thinking of? Parade belongs with Jim Silver, and he's going back to his master."

"Julie, you're going to ride home on Parade," said Clonmel. "I'm taking half a day off, Bill," he added to me.

The girl went up to the stallion with her hand held out, palm up. The big horse snorted and lunged back until Clonmel caught him and drew him gently forward.

"You have to have an introduction," he said to Julie. "Stand there, and then I'll bring him up to you."

He did that, talking softly, soothing the stallion with his hand, until presently the chestnut and the girl were face to face. They made a fine picture, each as splendid a specimen as the other, each of them trembling with excitement.

It was a queer thing to hear her talk to him, panting.

"I'd give—half my life—to ride you—a mile, Parade!"

Then she got her hand on his face, and he drew back, and was again drawn forward, and finally permitted her touch to remain there.

And five minutes later she sat there in the saddle, frightened but delighted, while Clonmel explained what she should do. There was only a light hackamore on the head of Parade. Men said that only once had a bit been between his teeth. It was folly to try to rule him by force of hand, therefore. A loose rein and a gentle touch, however, might make him go as smoothly as the wind.

As I watched her start to pace Parade gently up and down, talking to him in a quieting voice, risking the unchainable force of him on the lightness of her own hands, my heart kept on sinking.

Charlotte said to me suddenly: "You go along with them. Something is bound to happen. Bill Avon, you've got to see it through—whatever it is. Go along, with them!"

I knew that that was right. I went out and caught up a horse and saddled it. By that time, the pair had started across the plain toward the pass that split through the mountains beside Mount Craven, and the wolf still skulked on the lead rope beside the stallion, pulling out as far as the rope would let him go.

I kept a good distance to the rear, because those two gay young people probably had a lot to say to one another, and a lot of admiration to shed out of their eyes. I must say that they made a good picture as they drifted ahead of me. Now they were cantering their horses, and I could see them turning their heads, while fragments of their laughter blew back to me. It was all very young and fine, but the devil would be to pay before long, I was sure.

It was like opening a play which has some very gay first chapters, but whose label is tragedy.

6 / At the Cary Place

THE PASS WAS always a dreary place, but on this day it was more weird than ever, with the tag ends of the storm still blowing in tatters through the gulch, and the flash and quick rushing of water down the cliffs and across the floor of the ravine. The whole thing had a wet gleam, as though it had just been heaved out of an ocean. It was like a bit of new world making, and when I glanced ahead at Clonmel and the girl, I could not help feeling that they were the sort of people to inhabit big, new spaces. They had the spirit for it. As for me, too much dust was in my nostrils.

I kept trailing along behind them until they were through the pass and coming right down on the outskirts of the town of Blue Water. And still they were so wrapped up in one another that they never turned their heads to see what might be coming behind them.

As we got nearer the town, where the trails braided together into a wagon road, I saw a number of people come out from the byways and from the scattering of houses, and in every case they seemed to be stunned by the appearance of the stallion on which the girl was riding.

I cantered up to the pair at last, when they were getting close to the Cary house, where Julie lived as the ward of Dean Cary. She was also engaged to Dean's son, Will Cary, as she had told Clonmel the night before. But as I stared at the pair of them, I could not help thinking that the engagement now stood on most precarious feet.

As I came up, big Clonmel sang out to me, not at all surprised that I was there:

"Look at the way she's handling Parade, Bill!"

I regarded the horse and the girl jealously. Jealously, because a hero is a property of every ordinary man and

35

because of such men as Jim Silver the rest of us stand straighter. He was a man who had never been found in a cruel, mean, or cowardly action. He had never been beaten by equal odds. He had dared to measure himself against the cunning and the forces of the great Barry Christian. And Silver had built himself into a sort of kingship, with this throne naturally on the back of the great golden chestnut, Parade. It was as though Julie, with her slender brown hands, had dethroned the hero and dared recklessly to take his place. And as I looked at her and then at Clonmel, I almost hated the pair of them. I would have given a vast deal to learn what had happened up there in the woods on the side of the great mountain when Clonmel surprised Silver and mastered him.

That was one of the chief parts of the marvel—that Silver could have been surprised, for with Parade and Frosty on guard, it was popularly supposed that every scent and sound of approaching danger must instantly be translated for the benefit of the master. Yet it must have been by surprise that Clonmel had managed to overwhelm that famous fighter. Once his grasp was well lodged on Jim Silver—yes, then it would be understandable that any man in the world might have become helpless!

Gloomily I regarded the manner in which Parade went gently along under the girl. She made no effort to keep him firmly in hand, but let him move under a free rein, his head turning here and there as he took note of all around him, his splended body shimmering in the morning light as he danced along.

"You don't like the look of Julie or Parade?" asked Clonmel of me.

"It makes a pretty picture. I hope it's not spoiled before long," said I. "But isn't that the Cary house, yonder?"

It was the Cary place, all right, distinguished by the number of big trees that grew around it—so many that the ax had not been able to clear away the majority of them for firewood. As we came up the trail through the trees, a dozen or so boys from Blue Water rattled out of town on their ponies and stopped with a yell, to look after Parade and Frosty like so many Indians. They did not follow on, which surprised me till I remembered the rather grim reputation which the Cary family had all through the mountains. They were people who kept to themselves and demanded their privacy.

We got through the trees and saw the ranch house, as ugly and sprawled out and shapeless and unpainted as most of our ranch houses are. The rough-hewn stumps of many trees surrounded the place; the ground was littered with chips, big and small, rotten-yellow or gleaming white. One monster of a tree had been felled not long before and had been only half worked up for firewood. Part of the trunk was propped up on a section of log, and a big crosscut saw had been left sticking in a new cut. You could tell that the Cary outfit did only as much work around the place as had to be done; they were people to labor with their cattle, not with their homes.

Dean Cary sat on a stump near the door of the house. He was as big, almost, as Harry Clonmel, and the shaggy gray of his fifty years made him seem even larger. There were tales about Dean Cary that cooled the blood a good deal, but those tales dealt with a time two decades away, which in the West is enough to quite bury an old life and let a new growth spring out of the wreckage.

He was smoking a long-stemmed pipe with a bowl of the red Indian pipestone, and he kept on puffing and looking at us and through us, while we came up. He did not rise. He gave us no greeting. When we were almost on him, he simply took the pipe from his mouth and bellowed:

"Will!"

We halted and got off the horses as Will Cary came out from the house. What a man he was, big as an elk and as fit for speedy motion! He was a handsome man. You would have said that there was a strong dash of Indian blood in him, to judge by the swarthy glow of his skin. He was so handsome in feature that he possessed a certain nobility which might degenerate later on, if one could judge by the indications about the eyes.

Will Cary walked out to us two steps, saw Parade and Frosty, and turned to stone. That's exactly the word for it—he changed to a statue in the act of striding, about to lift foot from the ground. That was a fine picture to see—

37

the amazement in that big fellow so great that it resembled fear. Perhaps it *was* fear, because I could understand why he turned his head and his eyes probed swiftly, guiltily, among the trees. He was looking for the sign of the master, Jim Silver. He could only get hold of himself little by little.

Dean Cary did not want peace in the air, it seemed, because he growled: "Here's a couple of strangers bringin' home your girl to you, Will!"

But that leading remark was wasted for the moment. Will Cary gave hardly a glance at the girl except to exclaim:

"Parade and Frosty! Where did they come from?"

"From Jim Silver, of course," answered Julie Perigord. "Harry Clonmel, here, got them away from Silver."

"Got them away—from Jim Silver!" breathed Will Cary.

His eyes stared at the heels of Clonmel and they widened slowly as he looked up toward the head of the giant. After all, there was not such a deal of difference in the size of that pair, but what Will Cary had just heard was enough to make him see nightmares in the flesh. I could sympathize with that feeling.

But old Dean Cary exclaimed: "That's a lie! That young feller never took nothin' from Jim Silver. If he got the hoss and the wolf, he got 'em by a cheat!"

Clonmel turned quickly, saw the gray hair of the speaker, and then shrugged his shoulders. Will Cary was greatly embarrassed. He said:

"Stop that sort of talk, will you, Dad? You folks come in a while. We'll put Parade in the barn, and Frosty along with him. Jumping thunder, what a horse! I never saw him as close as this. Look at those quarters, Dad. He could carry three hundred pounds all day long. Carry it like a feather in the wind. Come on back and we'll put Parade in the barn."

We went around behind the house. There was a haze over my mind. I walked in a dream. Something bad was going to happen—I couldn't tell what. Pretty soon, Will Cary would stop wondering about the stallion and Frosty and begin to realize that his girl had been brought home by another man. Then action was apt to start. And if

Clonmel was the bigger of the two, Will Cary knew ways of cutting almost any man down to his own size. And as I walked along with the rest and heard them chattering, my mind turned back to Jim Silver and the surety with which Dean Cary had said that no man could take anything away from Silver. It was the feeling that everyone seemed to have—that Silver was invincible.

How, then, had Clonmel taken that horse away from the fighter? If it had been a trick, how had he managed to trick that crafty veteran of a thousand battles?

I decided hat the best thing was to stop thinking and let the future take care of itself, but every moment, I expected to hear the noise of a galloping horse and to see Jim Silver breaking out from the big, dark circle of the trees.

We put Parade in a stall in the barn. Frosty lay down exactly under the feet of the stallion and dropped his head on his paws. He looked like a perfectly tame dog, except that the eyes which watched us were green. Looking at the size of him and at his eyes, it was easy to remember that once a bigger price had been put on the scalp of that cattle killer than was usually laid on the head of a human murderer.

Will Cary stood back to admire the picture the two made, for a moment.

"Look at 'em!" he said under his breath, after he had poured some crushed barley into the feed box. "Parade won't eat the stuff I offer him. The grain and the hay don't mean a thing to him unless his boss is around to see him eat it. Think of having a pair like that ready to die for you, watch for you, fight for you! Think of it!"

Well, I was already thinking of it, dizzily.

Will took us back into his house. He brought out a jug of moonshine that I wouldn't drink, but Clonmel took a big swig of it.

"How did you do it, partner?" asked Will Cary. "How did you get 'em away from Silver?"

"Silver's not dead," answered Clonmel, "and according to your father, it must have been a cheat."

Cary frowned. He leaned forward in his chair and stared at Clonmel for a moment, with doubt in his eyes.

Then he said: "And how do you happen to be gadding around with strangers, Julie?"

"That's *my* business," said the girl calmly.

Her eyes flashed from one of those big men to the other. I had been liking her a good deal, up to that time, but now it seemed to me that I could see a big touch of animal in her—the sort of thing that makes a woman glad to see two men fighting for her. Like a she-wolf, she might go to the stronger.

I commenced to say that we'd better be starting on home, when old Dean Cary walked into the room, his cowhide boots creaking, and mutter:

"Come out with me for a minute, Will!"

Will got up and followed his father from the room. The rest of us sat there in a silence that thickened and deepened, and I knew that the trouble I had been dreading was only moments away.

7 / Silver's Friend

IN THOSE MOMENTS that followed, my eyes went vaguely around the room. It had been a parlor once. It had been that in the days of Mrs. Cary, no doubt, and there was still a faded, flowered carpet on the floor, and a round mahogany table in the center of the room, and a few family photographs growing dim behind their glass along the wall; but harness hung from pegs, fishing rods leaned in a corner, initials had been whittled into the edge of the table, and spurs had scarred the top of it. It was woman-made, that room, but it had been manhandled.

Julie said, with a darkening face, finally: "There's something in the air. What is it?"

"There's something in the air. We'd better get out of here," said I. "We'd better go home."

"No," broke in Clonmel, "I'm not leaving for a while."

He looked at the girl. She flushed under his eye and

was about to speak, but before a word came from her, a shadow stepped noiselessly into the open doorway at the front of the room. I thought for a dizzy moment that it might be Silver himself. Then I saw that it was a fellow of only average height, very slenderly made—a wonderfully handsome, dark-eyed man with a pale skin and black hair. The lids drooped over his eyes. He had less the appearance of one looking at us than of one listening to distant sounds.

But I knew instantly that he was keenly aware of all of us. An air of the town clung to him. He wore an ordinary range outfit, but it was not in place on him. It looked as though it had been hand-worked by an expensive tailor in imitation of the swaggering clothes of the range.

"You rode in on Parade," said he to Julie, without any form of greeting. "Where did you get him?"

I glanced at the girl and saw that she was out of her chair and standing stiff and straight without a whit of color in her face. She was frightened out of her breath, and that was plain. But five minutes before, I would have sworn that not even the charge of a grizzly bear would trouble her.

"I don't know," she stammered. "I don't know where I got him—Taxi!"

The name ripped right through me. I stared again at him and saw his eyes lift a little. They were pale eyes, brighter than any I had even seen. People said that once a man had looked into the eyes of Taxi, he would never forget them. I could understand that now. At that instant, with a quiet fury rising in him, he looked like a pale and dressed-up devil, ready for a kill.

And that was what he was ready for—murder! You could tell it in the stillness of his attitude, in something about the slender, nervous hands, and above all, in the pale glare of his eyes. Murder—because we had crossed the trail of Jim Silver, and Silver was his friend. Men said that Taxi had come out of the underworld and had been caught and changed and made over by Silver. At any rate, it was true that the friendship between them was legendary all through the mountain desert.

"You don't know where you got Parade?" asked Taxi, in his soft, gentle, deadly voice.

"Here!" exclaimed Clonmel. "I gave her Parade to ride, and what the devil of it?"

"Ah," said Taxi. "*You* got Parade for her, did you?"

"Yes, I got him, and—"

"Harry, be still!" said the girl. "You don't know what you're doing. It's Taxi—"

"He knows what he's doing. Any man who can get Parade knows exactly what he's doing. He's stealing."

Then he added, his voice even gentler than before: "He's a low, sneaking thief, to begin with."

"Why, you little rat," said Clonmel, "if you were a foot taller and twice your weight, I might have to take a fall out of you for that!"

"I suppose you might," said Taxi. "I'm standing here waiting for you to try."

He smiled, and the red tip of his tongue slid across his lips. Oh, if ever I saw a calm devil, Taxi was the man at that moment.

"Don't budge, Harry!" shrilled the girl.

She jumped in front of him and hooked her arms back through his, while she faced Taxi. Up over her shoulder she pleaded with Clonmel.

"Don't move a hand, or he'll kill you, Harry. He's Silver's best friend!"

"Steady, Taxi," said I. "I'm with Clonmel. I want to explain—"

"Then I'll have to take my chances with the pair of you," said Taxi. "A horse thief is my idea of a snake. I'm telling you that, whoever you may be."

Taking chance with the pair of us? Why, men said that there was hardly a hair's-breadth of difference between the skill of Silver and Christian and Taxi, when it came to guns. We were as good as dead the instant that a gun was drawn.

Therefore, guns must not be drawn, in spite of the fact that Clonmel was saying through his teeth:

"Julie, stand away from me, or I'll have to lift you away."

"Don't move!" she begged. "The instant I'm away from you, he'll kill you, Harry. It's Taxi! It's Taxi! Can't you understand that?"

"Julie," said Clonmel, "if you don't—"

At that, far, far away, like a trumpet blowing small on the horizon, a stallion neighed. The sound was not muffled by walls, but by thin distance alone.

The effect on Taxi was like the blow of a whip. He literally jumped.

"It's Parade!" he exclaimed. "Who's got him now?"

"It can't be Parade. He's safe in the barn," said Clonmel.

"Safe in the barn? Safe for Barry Christian in the barn, I suppose you mean," said Taxi savagely. "You are with the Cary outfit. You've all thrown in with Christian. But two of you are going to step out of the picture this minute. Fill your hands!"

Without lifting his voice he had put the cold acid right on my heart. I made a vague gesture, tugging at my Colt. Big Clonmel swept the girl away from before him with a single motion. She was screaming, and Clonmel was leaning to rush bare-handed at the gunman, while Taxi, with an automatic hip-high, was covering me and ready to fire.

He wanted to shoot, mind you. I never saw a more devilish eagerness to kill in any face. But he checked himself. The violence of his impulse was so great that it swayed his entire body forward. What it was that stopped him, I could not make out at first, but instead of trying to free my own gun, I let it lie, half exposed, and heard Taxi snarl:

"You half-wit, where's your gun!"

"Damn a gun!" said Clonmel, and charged like a bull.

My own Colt fell to the floor. I simply made a dive at Clonmel and hit him low enough to knock him off balance, so that the pair of us crashed in the corner.

When my wits cleared, the girl was in front of Taxi, begging. Clonmel was getting up slowly, and he pulled me to my feet by the nape of my neck. It was the queerest scene I ever saw, and the most nervy. But somehow, I knew that my dive at Clonmel had kept him from being shot through the head.

He knew it, too, now that he had been given a few seconds to think things over. I heard Taxi saying to the girl:

"I'm not going to shoot the fool! But—where's Parade now? Where have the Cary outfit put him?"

"He's in the barn. With Frosty. They're both out there," said Julie.

"We're going out to have a look," remarked Taxi. "The rest of you walk ahead of me."

We went ahead of him, fast enough. I was hurrying, but I couldn't keep up with the huge strides of Clonmel, who kept muttering:

"Suppose he should be gone! Suppose he should be gone!"

He reached the door of the barn and almost tore it off its running rail in his haste to get it open. We looked into the dimness and the pungency of the interior, and there was no trace of the glimmering beauty of Parade, no token of the dusty gray of the wolf.

"He's gone!" said Clonmel. His voice rose with an agony. "Bill, what can I do about it? Where have they taken him?"

"To Barry Christian," answered Taxi. "They need money, and they know that Christian will pay the price they ask if he can put his hands on the stallion and the wolf."

He turned around on Clonmel and said to him:

"You've cut the heart out of Jim Silver—you've stolen his ears and his eyes and the speed that used to snake him across the mountains like a bird through the sky. You've sunk a knife in him—and I can't pay you off for it! I've got to stand here and look at a fool and let him live!"

He was sick with rage; he looked sick. So did big Clonmel, for one thing. But Harry Clonmel made a gesture to the sky and shook his fist at the clouds.

"I'll keep the trail till I get Parade back!" he said. "I'll keep it till I've brought him safely back to Jim Silver!"

"Safely back—for Silver?" asked Taxi. "Did you say that?"

"I said that," answered Clonmel. "D'you think that I'd

get him for myself? If you know Jim Silver, don't you know well enough that he's only a borrowed horse?"

"Borrowed horse!" shouted Taxi. "I'm going crazy! You might get Parade from Silver by fighting or by stealing—but whoever heard of borrowing a man's hands and feet, and his ears and eyes? Because that's what Parade and Frosty have been to Jim. Borrowed Parade?"

"Yes," said I. "That's exactly what he must have done."

"Then I'm out of my wits," muttered Taxi, "and the world's not what it used to be. But—you're telling the truth—you've borrowed him! Well, go borrow Jim Silver to help us out on the trail. We're apt to need him."

"Go and confess that I've lost his horse for him?" groaned Clonmel, in such a voice that I was ashamed with him. "Well, I'll even do that, if I have to. Bill, are you going to help me?"

"I'll help you," I said gloomily, because I dreaded the future that was breathing cold down my spine already.

"Three men on a trail!" said Clonmel, "and one woman left behind them to talk, and talk, and stab them in the back."

"I won't talk, Harry," said Julie Perigord. "I'll be as still as stone. I won't say a word to Dean Cary or Will —but it's not true that they've thrown in with Barry Christian! They've never even mentioned his name. They—"

"You fished for Parade to give him to the Carys," said Clonmel bitterly. "You've done their dirty work, and ruined me. I hope I never get sight of you again!"

And he turned away and left her.

8 / Taxi's Arrangements

SOMEONE SHOULD HAVE said a word for Julie Perigord, and I was the one to have spoken and told Clonmel that he was acting brutally when he talked to her as he did, but I was too much taken up by our own troubles, and that was why the three of us walked away from her white, sick face. I had heard the name of Barry Christian linked up with that of the Cary family, and I knew that if we were matching ourselves against such a combination as that, we were just about beaten at the start. I let the troubles of poor Julie slip out of my mind, while the three of us pulled back into the trees with our horses and sat down in the shade to think.

There was no use trying to follow the trail while it was hot, we decided, because the men who traveled with Parade were going like the wind, and they would keep on going like that until they reached some of the stone-paved ravines among the hills, where no sign of the flight would be printed on the ground. We had to think our way to a conclusion, reach far enough ahead with our wits to find where Parade might be taken.

First of all, I suggested that Will Cary admired the stallion so much that he might very well have stolen him for his own uses, but Taxi shook his head. He said that the Carys would never dare to bring down the anger of Jim Silver unless they had strong backing, and the only backing that would seem strong enough would be that of Barry Christian, who had carried on his struggle with Silver during so many years.

"But what makes you think that Christian is in this part of the world?" asked Clonmel.

"What else brought Jim Silver here?" asked Taxi sadly. "What else keeps him traveling across the world, jumping here and jumping there, never easy? What else brings me trailing along behind him, trying to help, only in touch with him once in a long while, because he doesn't want me in on the danger that always lies ahead? No, Silver is up here somewhere, because he thinks that Christian is around. And the Cary outfit is one that used to play into Christian's hand a long time ago. They're probably playing into the same hand now. People that have had his easy money don't forget the taste of it very soon. He'll pay them thousands for Parade. Why shouldn't he?"

It was clear enough as an argument, after all, and I knew the legend that Silver had sworn never to rest until, at last, he ran Barry Christian to the ground. I listened

46

to the lonely wind in the trees and felt cold in spite of the warmth of the day.

"Well," I said, "I'm willing to do what I can. But I don't know what we can manage—the three of us against the lot of them."

"One of us has to go and take the word to Silver," Clonmel said. "The other two ought to watch here, because Will Cary and his father are sure to return. When they're back, if we can lay hands on one of them, we may make him show us the way to Parade—and Christian, if Christian is there."

"The Carys won't come back—not for a long time," said Taxi. "They know that they're spotted. They're more apt to return to the hang-out of their whole clan."

"Where's that?" asked Clonmel.

"Back through the hills," said Taxi. "I don't know where. The old father of Dean Cary is still alive, and he's kept a tribe of sons and grandsons around him. Enough to turn back even Jim Silver. No, after Dean gets the horse to Christian, he'll go back to his tribe."

"I know where they live," said I, the picture of the valley growing up suddenly in my mind. "It's just under timber line. I could show the way, but—"

I hesitated, thinking of the number and the fierceness of those Cary men. I knew a lot about them.

Taxi asked for a description of the trail, and I drew a map of the route on the ground and pointed out the first landmarks, because we could see the mountains through the trees. It was arranged—Taxi did the arranging—that he and Clonmel should take the mountain trail until they had arrived close to the Cary clan. In the meantime, I was to fetch a course overland to the pass beside Mount Craven and try to locate Jim Silver. Clonmel told me where he had managed to find the great man. The reason I was sent toward Silver and not toward the Cary outfit was plainly that I was not much of a fighting man, and the Cary tribe might use their claws on strays that happened into their vicinity. Anyway, I got my horse and pounded away for the pass.

It was fixed that if I got hold of Silver, the two of us were to show up near the Cary place and fetch a course down the creek that flowed near it. Somewhere on the way we would come in hail of Taxi and Clonmel.

That was the background behind me when I climbed my mustang through the pass again, bound for Jim Silver. The day had been bright and hot in the valley, but up there in the country of the winds the sky was patched with racing clouds that kept drawing rapid pencil lines of shadow across the map.

I found the creek that worked among the trees in a shallow little ravine. I took the south side of that ravine, just as I had been instructed, and rode on among the pines, with the mustang slipping a good bit over the layered pine needles, until I came bang on the place which had been described to me by Clonmel as the site of the camp of Silver. It was the exact picture, with a big pine between two smaller ones, near the bank of the creek, and the face of the big tree shattered by lightning. But there was no trace of any campfire, no blackened soil, no dark spot of ashes, and no suggestion of broken firewood anywhere around.

After I had looked for a few moments, I began to feel that Clonmel must have seen the place, to be sure, but that nothing but ghosts had been in it.

I was still staring around when a voice said, behind me:

"Well, stranger?"

I jerked about in the saddle. There at the edge of a huge boulder was a tall fellow who reminded me of someone I had seen before. He had big shoulders and the legs and hips of a running stag. There was something about his brown face, too, that reminded me of other features which I could not place.

"Jim Silver!" I exclaimed.

"Who sent you up here?" he asked.

"Clonmel," said I.

"Ah, he sent you, did he?" answered Silver. "I think that's the last thing that—Clonmel would do."

He said this in rather a queer way. I felt that I had to establish the facts at once before he would believe me, and I blurted out:

48

"He only sent me back here because Parade and Frosty are gone. They've been stolen!"

He came up to me with quick steps and gripped the reins of my horse just under the chin, as though steadying the head of the mustang would hold me in a better place to be looked at.

"Parade? Frosty?" he echoed.

"They're gone!" I said wildly. I made a big pair of gestures to explain how entirely they were gone. The gestures also helped me to look away from the bright, grim eyes on this man. "Dean Cary and his son took them, while Harry Clonmel and I were in the house. Taxi heard about a stranger riding Parade. He came to the Cary place to fight to get them back for you. But instead of fighting, we went out to look in the barn—and the horse was gone."

I told him rapidly about what had happened and what plans we had made, while he backed a little away from me and released the head of the mustang.

I couldn't help winding up by crying: "But how did Harry Clonmel get the horse and the wolf away from you?"

"That's another matter," said Jim Silver. "The item for you to be interested in is that you're not riding back there with me."

"No?" said I. "You mean that you want my horse? Why, you can have him, Silver. All of us in these mountains—all the honest men—are willing to give you more than a horse if it will help. You take the mustang, and I'll peg along on foot. I may get there late, but I'll arrive."

He smiled at me a little.

"I'll get there on foot faster than any horse could take me," he said. "Any horse except one," he added. "But you're not for this sort of business. You're not trained to the minute for a fight, and there's apt to be fighting up there. I'll cut straight across the mountains, where a horse couldn't go, and I'll be at the headwaters of that creek before an ordinary mustang would carry me there. But you —you're going back home to your wife."

"Wife?" said I. "How do you know that I'm married?"

He smiled again.

"A woman sewed that patch at your knee," he said.

"Men don't take such small stitches or such regular ones. I'm grateful to you for wanting to help—but you're going home."

Now, as I stood there and looked at Jim Silver, I had a strange experience. I knew, in a flash, that all I had ever heard about him was true—all of his wild adventures, and all of his courage, and his steel-cool hardness of nerve. Invisible lips were calling to me, and I felt cold-hearted and alone in a strange way. I made a foolish and childish gesture toward him.

"My wife—she saw you once," said I, "and if she were here, she'd send me kiting along to help you. Yes, and she'd want to go along with us!"

I laughed, but Jim Silver did not laugh. He just looked at me.

"I've got to go," I said at last. "I'd never have the courage to call my soul my own, if I didn't go. I'd never be able to face my son."

He kept his silence until I thought it would never end, and at last he said:

"If anything happens to you—"

"I have a son to carry on after me and work the ranch," said I. "I've got to go, Silver."

He walked slowly up to me again, and raised his face so that I could see a sort of gentleness and sadness in it. He took my hand.

"I don't even know your name," he said.

"Bill Avon," I said, "and—"

"Bill Avon," said Silver, and gave my hand a good, long grip.

I could feel that the strength of that grasp had sealed us together, and I wished that he had given me the grip after I had done something worth while, not before. I had the uneasy feeling of a man who has been paid in advance for goods that have not been delivered and that will be hard to find.

When he stepped away from me, he said:

"That pony has done some hard traveling today. You'll do better by him and yourself if you unsaddle here and let him rest an hour or so. Give him a drink and cool him off. After that, you can ride as fast as you please on the trail. And another thing—will your wife be breaking her heart when you don't turn up at home?"

I thought of Charlotte and drew in a long, slow breath. "No," I said shortly. "She won't be breaking her heart!"

9 / The Cary Domain

IT WAS NOT a great deal after noon of that day before I got around the half circle of riding that I had to complete before I was near the hang-out of the Cary clan. Grandfather Cary had his head about him when he picked out that spot. It was a little mountain kingdom all of its own. The mountains fenced it around in a circle. Half a dozen creeks flowed down through it. The forests came off the highlands and slipped in green floods over the valleys, and where the forests ended, the grazing land began, pushing out arms among the woods and extending over a great central portion of the plateau where there were only occasional groves of trees. In one of those groves was the old Cary house.

Almost any other people in the world would have become rich with such a domain to exploit, but the Carys could not accumulate wealth so long as "Old Man" Cary lived. And he seemed to defy death like a stone. Time could crack and wear and seam and color him, but it could not rub him out.

Old Man Cary possessed a queer cross between faith in God and hatred of man. He refused to take ordinary precautions. He refused to build the big barns and feeding yards where a great herd of cattle could be sheltered when bad winters came along—and, of course, bad winters came pretty frequently at that altitude. But when the thermometer dropped toward zero and often dipped below it, Old Man Cary shrugged his shoulders and left everything to the will of God. That was why the big Cary herd would increase for half a dozen seasons and then half of it would

51

be wiped out. The bones lay heaped, here and there. I saw a whole white windrow of them under the edge of a bluff against which hundreds and hundreds of beeves had been driven by a fierce blizzard and where they had stood until they froze. That had been many years before, but the same disaster had happened over and over again. And he would look around through his family to find out a recent sin which the Lord might be punishing.

There were plenty of sins to be found. A few of his descendants, like Dean Cary, had left the home preserve and founded homes here and there, but the majority of them preferred to remain in the land of their inheritance. They were all slaves of the old man's word, and he had plenty of words. He said when cattle could be driven to market, and that was the moment when they had to be taken out, no matter what the state of the market might be. He said when and how much timber should be felled for the winter store of wood. He named the creeks that could be fished and the ones where the stock must be allowed to accumulate. Now and then he would step down into the more intimate details and invade the privacy of the home of one of his sons or grandsons, and the terrible old fellow was sure to leave scars wherever he struck.

It was, on the whole, a wild and easy life for his offspring, of course. They had plenty of beef and fish; they could dig vegetables out of the vegetable patch; their horses were a splendid big race of animals; they were all allowed to spend a share of the cash income on clothes and foolishness; plenty of moonshine whisky was made on the place, and for houses they built on crooked wings and sprawling additions to the great log cabin of the old man. On the whole, it was a life for wild Indians. The only modern improvements that the old man permitted were the big steel locks on the doors.

I thought of these things when I came down from the headwaters of the creek, along which I expected to find Clonmel, and Silver, and Taxi. I was thinking so busily about them that I ran into a whang of trouble. I rode around a bend of the stream and heard a voice croak at me, and saw a young Cary pointing his rifle at my head.

I don't think he was more than fifteen. His brown

spindle shanks were only half covered by ragged overalls with half a pair of suspenders to hold them up. His shirt was a sun-faded rag of blue and white. His head stuck up like a big fist on a lean, sinewy forearm. But he was a Cary, all right. I could tell it by the black of his shaggy hair and by the black of his bright eyes. I could tell it by something fiercely unrelenting in his manner, which made him seem eager to treat me as he would have treated a wolf or a deer. Men told strange tales of things that had happened up here beyond the law. This lad had bare feet and a fine new repeating rifle. That was what you would expect in a Cary. They were men who didn't know how to miss with a gun, whatever else they might miss in life.

"Who are you, stranger?" he asked.

"My name is Bill Avon," said I.

"What are you doing up here?" he asked.

"Looking for some cattle to buy," said I.

"Ain't the time of year we sell cows," said he. "You know that."

"No, I don't know that," said I.

"Why would you wanta buy cows here?"

"Because I've heard that they can be bought cheap."

"Where do you live?"

"Away over there between Blue Water and Belling Lake. I've got a ranch."

"Yeah?" said the boy.

He kept the rifle on me. There was no let-up in the fierce brightness of his eyes, the cruelty in them. Something kept pulling at his mouth, and it was not kindness that kept it twitching. Young people like to kill for the sake of killing, and this lad was not only young but he was a Cary.

The story was that no one was an acceptable member of the clan until he had killed his man. It was certain that all the young men left Cary Valley and journeyed here and there through the West. About half of them or more never came back. Those who returned wore scars, as a rule.

I have even heard it said that every single male in Cary Valley had killed his man. This I don't vouch for, but it's a common superstition among a lot of people who ought to know what they're talking about. No wonder my flesh was creeping more than a little as I faced this young savage.

He kept turning the idea of me in his mind like a bird on a spit.

"You go on with your hunting, and I'll ride on and see your folks," said I.

He grinned at me.

"You think I'm a fool. You're a fool for thinking so," said he.

"What's your name?" I asked him.

"Chuck," said he.

"Chuck," said I, "you ought not to look at a stranger as though he were a freak of nature or a snake. What's wrong about a fellow riding into your valley?"

"Nobody's asked here; nobody's wanted here; nobody but a fool or a crook would try to break in," said Chuck. out."

"All right, then," said I patiently. "If that's the way you people feel about it, I'll have to turn around and get out.'

"Yeah. Go on and git," said Chuck.

I turned the horse, glad to be headed away from that young panther.

"Wait a minute!" he sang out.

I pulled the reins and turned my head.

"Maybe I'll take you on to the house," said he.

"That suits me," said I.

"Maybe it won't suit you so well when the old man gets through with you," said Chuck. "Ride alone ahead of me, and don't try no funny business, or I'm goin' to lambast you."

I rode ahead of him and I didn't try any funny business. But I could hardly keep from chuckling when I thought of the trouble that lad had ahead of him if he kept right down this side of the creek. Taxi and Silver and Clonmel were all down there, somewhere, waiting for me. It would probably be quite a point in this lad's life, if he had a close look at the great Jim Silver.

We went a good mile down the creek before he called out to me to stop.

"There's a right good ford here," he said, "and we'll cross over to the other side of the creek."

That spoiled my plans. It was on the south side of the creek that I expected to meet my three friends.

"What's the matter with riding along here?" I asked him.

"I dunno," he said, "except that you come in on this trail, and maybe it'll be a pile better if we hit across on the other side and take *my* trail."

I was amazed as well as disappointed. The boy had the suspicions of a wild beast, and in this case they were justified.

I crossed the ford and he came along after me. The water got up as high as the knees of my horse, and once I figured on turning suddenly back at Chuck. But a glimpse of the bright black eyes and the lean, stern young face, and the way the rifle was constantly at the ready changed my mind for me.

I crossed that ford, and a moment later we were heading off on a trail among the trees, and leaving the little ravine of that creek far behind us.

I knew then that I was not destined to see Silver and the rest before I saw the inside of the Cary house. Thank Heaven, that was all I *did* know of what was lying ahead of me.

10 / The Head of the Clan

WE LEFT THE TREES and entered the big central plain of the Cary Valley until we hit a maze of old and new trails that had been worn by cattle and horses, and then we came in sight of the Cary house, spilling out right and left behind its screen of trees.

I could see cattle dotting the plain, here and there,

little single points, or whole smudges of red. They were feeding on the finest grama-grass, the best fodder in the world for horse or cow, I believe. The cows we passed were sleek as butter and filled right up round between the short ribs and the hip bones.

We got up along another creek that came white with speed down the farther slope of the valley, close to the Cary house, and around a bend we came upon a lot of women washing clothes. They were standing in the water or crouching like Indians along the rocks, soaking, and rubbing, and beating the clothes, and using mighty little soap. That, in the days of good washing machines and scrubbing boards, and when even half-wits ought to know that clothes need boiling before they are really clean at all.

But I didn't wonder very much at the primitive methods of that laundry, because what staggered me was the look of the women themselves. I had seen a Cary woman here and there, but never a group of them, and what a set they were! They were all handsome, in a way, but built on heroic lines, with plenty of bone in body and face. Some of the young girls who were down there helping with the work were quite beautiful; time had not yet filled them out to the full Cary measure.

Every solitary one of those women had black hair and eyes. It was said that one of Old Man Cary's mandates was that he would have no blondes in his valley.

These big women all turned around and stared at us as wild creatures and brutal savages do, gaping, some of them, and never shifting their eyes, and laughing, and pointing me out. To be frank, they frightened me more than any group of men could have done. I mean, there was such cruelty in their eyes and such strength in their hands that they looked capable of anything.

The trail took us up to the home grove and through the trees to the front of the house. It was the sort of thing you would expect, just a bare flat of beaten ground with a hitching rack here and another one there, and a stone-paved run of water that went close to the front door, where the horses could be conveniently given drink. A dozen small youngsters were rolling around, playing. They got up and looked at us. They stared, and pointed me out silently.

"Hey! Hey, somebody!" yelled Chuck.

A woman came to the nearest door and screened her eyes against the slanting rays of the sun. She was a huge woman, swarthy, sun-darkened.

"What you want, Chuck?" he asked. "Who you gone and got there?"

"Shut your mouth and go and tell the old man I wanta see him," said Chuck.

"Yeah? All right," said she, taking no offense at this rough talk.

I could gather from the specimen that the men occupied a position of dignity in the valley, perhaps from the moment when they could daub a rope on a cow or go out and shoot venison. Anyway, the woman left the door, and I heard her begin to bawl out:

"Hey, there, Grandpa! Hey, Grandpa!"

Her voice passed into the distance, but I could still hear it shrilling, several rooms away.

The children came up and stood close about us, staring, silent. Their eyes were as old as the eyes of any of the grown people—just as bright and just as cruel. I had a feeling that if their parents were all killed, the children would be able to live in the woods and forage well enough with tooth and nail.

My apprehension grew all the time I waited out there. And when I thought of Silver and Taxi and Clonmel, it was small comfort. They would never miss me. They would simply think that I had lost my heart and preferred, at the last moment, to remember Silver's invitation to go home and leave the rest of the business to better hands than mine. Even if the three of them wanted to help me, what could they do? What could anyone do? Three? It would need thirty to break into this fort where man and woman and child were capable of hard battle.

And if Silver was a superman, still the Carys were close to being supermen, also.

Suddenly I saw that this den of wild beasts ought to be broken up and the inhabitants scattered. The law had never taken a single step past the flat, stone faces of that

57

circle of cliffs which fenced in the round of the plateau. It was time for it to appear.

I tried to talk to the boy. I said: "Chuck, do you fellows aim to bring in every stranger who happens to ride into the valley?"

"What would strangers be doin' up here?" he asked me brutally. "Nobody but a Cary has got no rights in this valley, I guess."

"So you put a gun on them and bring them in?"

He looked me slap in the eye, while his mouth twisted into a grin.

"Some of 'em won't be brung," he said. "Some of 'em would have to be left, I reckon."

Left dead, was what he meant. I needed no interpreter to tell me that much.

The big woman appeared in the doorway again.

"Take him around to the old man's room," she said. "He'll see him. Who is he, Chuck?"

"Calls himself Bill Avon and says he wants to buy cows. I dunno who he is," said Chuck.

To me he added: "Get off that hoss."

I dismounted, with the hollow eye of the rifle watching me with special care in case I should try any quick moves.

"Now march ahead of me," said Chuck.

He sent me around the side of the house and marched behind, and the silent, black-eyed children ran out ahead of me, turning and staring up at me over their shoulders, as children will when they march ahead of a band. There was no dignity of noise to this moment, but there was plenty of danger, and they wanted to see how I would take it. I was suddenly glad—gladder than I had ever been before in my life—that I was middle-aged, not at all imposing, and with a good record of long and honest work behind me.

When we turned the farther corner of the house, I saw a big vegetable garden stretching away to the next trees. Another runlet of water ran through it, and there were little mud embankments to contain the flood when it was poured on one patch or another. New green tops were pricking the black of the earth, here and there. I saw the

58

dirty yellow or ripe onions, ready to be dug up; tomato vines were growing up on frames, and off in the distance there was a woman bending over a broad-bladed hoe. The flash of it seemed to strike right into me.

The back of the house was more irregular than the front of it, because here big cabins or little ones had been added to the long structure and the rear showed the differences in size. Finally, we came to a door, where Chuck halted me. He kept his rifle in both hands and kicked the door.

"Who's there?" called a voice that was so husky and deep that it seemed one could count the number of vibrations per second that went to the make-up of the sound.

"Chuck. I got something to show you," said the youngster.

"Open the door and come in."

Chuck opened the door with his left hand, keeping the rifle carefully under his right elbow. But I had no intention of trying to escape. I felt as though I were in the center of a hostile kingdom—as though a great continent had swallowed me up.

I stepped through that doorway and found myself before Old Man Cary.

It was a naked sort of a room with nothing much to it except a broad open hearth and an iron crane hanging in it, with a black pot that hung from the crane, over the low welter of the fire. The smell of the cooking broth was stale through the room. Everything seemed to be soaked with the greasy odor, as though that same pot had been boiling there for years. Mutton was the smell, and if you know mutton, you know what I mean when I speak of the greasy rankness. The air was filled with it. Not this day's cooking only, but a stale offense that rose out of the ground and seeped out from the dark walls.

I say it came out of the ground because there was no wooden flooring. There was just beaten earth. Some of that earth was so footworn that it seemed to have a sheen about it, to my eyes.

Old Man Cary sat in a corner near the fire, with a rug pulled over his legs—an old, tattered, time-worn rug that was once the pelt of some sort of animal. Now, half the fur had been worn away. He had a broad bench beside him, and that bench was littered with revolvers and rifles which he was cleaning. I could imagine that he cleaned the guns for the entire clan and during that cleaning took heed of the way the different weapons had been used.

Now I hope you have some idea of what the place was like, but when it comes to Old Man Cary himself, it's hard to make a picture of him. He still had the great Cary frame which his descendants had inherited from him; he still sat as high as many a man stands. But there was no flesh on him. He was eaten away. Death had been at him for a long time and death was still at work. If it could not strike the old giant to the heart or the brain, it could at least worry him down little by little. His face had shrunk so that it seemed very small, unmatched to the size of his head, like a boy's face under a mature skull.

And his eyes were bright, sharp, young, under the wrinkling folds of the lids. He lifted those eyes to Chuck as he said:

"Who knocked at my door?"

"I did, Grandpa," said Chuck.

"You lie," said the old man. "You didn't knock. You kicked that door."

"Look," said Chuck. "I had my hands full of the gun, like this here, and I had to kind of rap the door with my foot."

"If you ever kick my door again," said that husky voice, which seemed to be tearing the fiber of the throat, "I'll nail you to a tree and take your hide off. Now, what you brought here to me?"

He turned his glance on me.

Chuck was so scared that he had to draw breath a couple of times before he could stammer out that I said my name was Bill Avon, that he had found me up the creek, and that I said I was coming to try to buy cattle, and that everybody ought to know that Cary cattle were not for sale at this time of year.

"They ought to know, ought they?" said the old man. "You know it, do you?"

"Yes, sir," said Chuck, more breathless than before.

"Cary cows are for sale when I say they're for sale. The time of the year don't make no difference," said the old man.

"Yes, sir," said Chuck. "I'm sorry."

"Sorry for what?"

"Sorry I didn't know."

"What didn't you know?"

"That the cattle—I mean—I dunno."

"You don't know what you don't know, eh? Are you a fool or ain't you a fool?"

"No, sir," said poor Chuck. "I mean—yes, sir."

"You got too much of your mother in you, and she's a fool woman. You hear me?"

"Yes, sir."

"You tell her that. Go back and tell her: 'Ma, you're a fool woman.' If she don't like that, send her to me, and I'll tell her some more."

"Yes, sir," said Chuck. "Pa would knock hell out of me if I told her that."

"You send your pa to me, too, then," said the old man. He looked at me. "You say you're Bill Avon, do you?"

"Yes," said I.

"You come to buy cattle?"

"Yes."

"How much money you got with you?"

"Fourteen, fifteen dollars."

"How many Cary cows would that buy?"

"I was going to dicker for a sale," said I.

"You're lyin'," said the old man. "Chuck, you was right to bring him in. You're a good boy. But what you mean by leavin' a gun on him? Take it away and fan him. We'll see what his linin' looks like!"

11 / Worse Trouble

THERE WAS NOTHING much to be done with that old devil. It was like talking to a man with an eye that could read the brain. I wondered what even the great Jim Silver would do if he ran up against a power like that of Grandpa Cary.

Grandpa went on cleaning a rifle and paying no attention until Chuck had heaped on an end of the bench everything from my pockets, plus the gun from my holster. There were some silver and a five-dollar greenback. There were my old pocket knife and wallet and some bits of string and a couple of nails. I always seem to have some nails around in my pockets, because you never can tell when nails will come in handy.

I stood there like a fool, in a sort of emptiness, waiting.

After Chuck had put my stuff on the bench, he stepped back and eyed me savagely. The rough things the old man had said to him were a grudge that the youngster passed along to me. That's the way with people bred to a certain level. As long as they can feel a good hate, they don't care in what direction it goes.

Before he paid any attention to me, the old man growled:

"M'ria!"

Maria popped a door open and stood on the threshold. She gave one flash at me, and then looked to the head of the clan for orders. She was not much older than Chuck and had not yet begun to bulge with the Cary brawn. She had big bare feet, and she would grow to the bigness of them, one day, but the rest of her was slim and round and smooth enough to stand in stone forever.

"M'ria, gimme somethin' to eat," said the old man.

She ducked back into the other room and came again

with speed enough to make her calico dress snap and flutter about her brown legs. She had a big pewter spoon, and a big earthenware bowl, and a lot of stale bread crusts dropped into the bowl. She took the cover off the pot above the fire and stirred the contents, and then dipped out enough of the broth, swimming with shreds of meat, to cover the crusts of bread.

She gave the old man the bowl, and he held it between his knees and began to eat. He was careless about his feeding, and he made a lot of noise at it. Sometimes the soup drizzled out of the corners of his mouth, and then the girl was quick as a wink to wipe the drops away before they had a chance to fall off his lean chin. He had no teeth, of course, and that compression of his lips was one thing that helped to make his face so small, and oddly boyish. Sometimes, too, he was so casual about the way he raised the spoon that some of the soup ran down over his hand and onto his hairy arm, and the girl was always there with an edge of her apron to keep him tidy.

When he had had all he wanted, he gave the bowl a shove. She took it at once. He put his bald old head back on the edge of the chair.

"You ain't a bad girl, M'ria," he said. "Gimme a kiss."

She leaned over him and kissed him on the lips. It must have been a little hard for her to do, but most youngsters are accomplished hypocrites if hypocrisy will give them advantage in the family.

"You make that soup pretty good, too," said the old man. "You make it better than that Alice ever done. I'm glad she gone and got married. Get out of here, now."

Maria got out. She had just time to pass one glance at Chuck, and the glint in her eyes said that she and Chuck knew each other fairly well. She was receiving sparks as well as passing them out, I should have said. When the door was closed after her, I was glad of the interruption. I was glad that the old man had some food to comfort his stomach while he talked to me. He got out a pipe and loaded it, and put it in his toothless mouth. He had a wad of blackened string wound around the stem of the pipe so that he could hold it better between his gums. He went on examining me.

"You bring up thirteen dollars and forty cents, and you're goin' to buy Cary cattle, are you?" he said.

"I brought along no money to buy. I wanted to see the cows and find out what the prices might be."

"How long you been around these parts?"

"I've had a ranch for about eight years."

"And you don't know that strangers ain't welcome in Cary Valley?"

"I don't know," said I. "Of course, I've heard that people don't come up here very much. Not most people. But I've seen some of the Cary cattle, and I wanted to buy some of them."

"You're a bright man. You got an education. A gent that's got an education is sure to be bright," said the old man, "and you stand there and try to tell me that you didn't know that you wasn't wanted up here?"

"I thought it was worth a chance," said I. "I didn't know, I can tell you, that you had gunmen out watching for strangers. But I'd seen the Cary cattle, and I wanted to buy some of them."

"Why did you want to buy 'em? Because they're so good?"

"No. They're not good. There's no size to them," I said.

"No? No size to my cows?" shouted the old man, suddenly enraged. And Chuck took a little hitch step toward me as though he were going to bash me in the face with his fist.

"There's no size to them. They're all legs," said I, "but they fat up well in a short season. If I could cross them on the short-legged breed I've got, I might manage to turn out a herd with size and one that fats up early in the season."

"You're a fool. He talks like a poor fool, Grandpa," said Chuck.

"Does he?" said that terrible old man. "If you was to listen to some fool talk like this, you might learn somethin', though. He's right. And doggone me if it ain't a

64

pleasure to hear sense talked once in a while, instead of the blatherin' blither I get up here, most of the time."

Chuck was pushed into the background of the conversation by this blast. The old man went on:

"You sound like you might have had a real business idea. But I dunno. It don't sound just right. You know you could 'a' got my cattle without ridin' clear up here. More'n once a year I send beef down to Blue Water and Belling Lake."

"I only got the idea the other day," said I.

The old man closed his eyes and smoked through a long moment.

"No," he announced at last. "You're lyin'. Doggone me if I wouldn't almost like to believe you. But I don't. Now, you come clean and tell me what really brought you up here."

"I've told you," said I.

"Yeah? You told me? Put up your hand and swear."

Well, I'm ashamed to say it, but I raised my right hand and swore. I think most of you would have done the same thing, if you'd been standing in my boots.

When I finished, Grandpa said:

"It ain't going to do. There's some folks, built along the lines of this gent, Chuck, that would rather put their hand into the fire than to swear a wrong oath, but he ain't quite that simple. No, sir, he's got more brains than that. He's got brains that I could talk to, I don't mind sayin'. But call in somebody. Call in Hugh, will you?"

You can see that I was in for trouble, already. The old man had looked pretty thoroughly through me. However, worse trouble was just ahead. Before Chuck could leave the room or sing out, we heard a door slam, and voices and heavy footfalls came toward us. Then there was a rap on the inside door of the room.

"Hey, Grandpa!" called the voice of Will Cary.

No, there was no mistaking it. The fine, deep ring of that voice carried a lot of conviction.

"Come in, Will," said the old man.

The door opened, and Will heaved in sight, with his father behind him, and Will sang out:

"Grandpa, what d'you think that we've landed for Barry—"

He snapped his teeth shut. He had not seen me, but his father had, and had silenced his son by the simple expedient of striking him a sharp blow across the back of his head, jarring his teeth together.

"Shut up, you dummy!" said Dean Cary, and pushed into the room, right toward me.

"What's this thing doin' here?" he demanded.

"Maybe you can help me out," said the old man. "I was just about to lock him up till I got some ideas about him."

"I can give you the ideas," said Dean Cary. "He's up here on the trail—of Parade and Silver's wolf. And that man-poisoning snake of a Taxi is probably up here somewhere, also. And then there's Silver himself who may be in the gang, and a man and a half by the name of Clonmel. You hear what I say? Silver—Taxi—and another —you hear me?" he shouted.

"Keep your voice down, I hear good, plenty," said the old man. "Seems like this one is tied up with important folks. But it always takes something big to make a man with brains get himself into trouble. You say there's a gent by the name of Silver? Who might he be?"

I was so astonished that I almost forgot my own danger. And then I saw that my own danger was more real than ever. For anything might happen in this place, this secluded valley where news of great Jim Silver had not arrived at the ears of the chief of the clan in all these years!

Dean Cary's breath was taken, too, so that the old man had a chance to ask again:

"And you talk about Parade, and Taxi, and Clonmel —even about a wolf. What have they to do with the Carys? And what did you start to say about Barry? Barry who? Barry Christian? Is that who you mean?"

Dean Cary looked at me with a calm balefulness in his eye. I had heard so much that I suppose he thought I might as well hear the rest of it.

"You know Barry Christian?" he said to his father.

66

"Doggone me if I ain't surprised. It's a whole lot for you to have heard about Barry Christian."

"Why, I've seen him, you fool," said the old man.

"You've seen him, have you? And you talked to him, did you?"

"Dean," said the head of the clan, "if I get any more of this kind of gab out of you, I'll have the whiskers tore off your face!"

"Why," shouted Dean Cary, "if you know Barry Christian, don't you know that he's been driven a dozen times out of one place after another by a devil on earth by the name of Jim Silver? Don't you know that Taxi is the name of Silver's friend? Don't you know that the pair of them have walked through hell together, and that they're able to walk through it again? And this fellow was with Taxi and Clonmel. This fellow is the spy the rest of 'em have sent ahead to look over the lay of the land!"

The old man rubbed his hands together, then took the pipe from his mouth.

"Seems like things is lookin' up a trifle, boys," said he. "Maybe the old blood is goin' to be warmed up a bit, eh? But if Silver is man enough to chase Barry Christian, then he's got more sense than to send a batty, half-blind gent like Bill Avon ahead of him for a spy. We'll talk it all over. Will, you and Chuck put Avon away and keep him safe and close."

12 / Barry Christian

THEY PUT ME IN the smoke-house, because it made as natural a prison as you'd wish to find. In order to keep the smoke in, it was windowless, with hardly a vent to it, and it was built of the heaviest sort of logs as though to make sure that the stocks of smoking meat could not be raised. It was a good-sized room, with a peaked roof and smoke-crusted crossbeams from which the cuts of meat could be hung. A side of bacon was still up there, I can't imagine why, and out of it seemed to come the reek of old curings and new that had soaked into the wood all around me. The smell was greasy. It seemed to fill the air like smoke until it made me breathless.

I sat down on the floor, as the heavy door was shut and locked on me. Things were getting pretty bad. I tried to think, but thoughts wouldn't come. I could only see pictures—of my home ranch and the look of the kitchen, buzzing with warmth and sweet with the smell of Charlotte's gingerbread on a cold winter evening.

There were a few chinks in the walls through which the light looked with eyes so small that the rays spread out in broken cones. But that light was a great deal better than the total darkness that began to gather as the day ended. For it made me think of my home ranch in another way, and of Charlotte stuffed and puffed with anger until her eyes were staring. She would never forgive me for this.

It was about this time that I heard the voice of Will Cary outside the smoke-house and then Julie Perigord, talking to him.

"He's in there. He's all right," said Will. "Come on away, Julie. I'd get the devil, if they knew that I'd showed you where he is."

"You *say* he's there," said Julie Perigord, "but how do I know?"

"D'you think that I'd lie to you?" asked Will.

I'll never forget what Julie said in answer.

"Oh, anyone would lie. We all lie. Half the things we say are lies. And this trouble is close to murder, Will. Of course you'd lie."

"You can't ask me to unlock a door when I haven't a key to it," said Will.

"You can let me rap on it and talk to him," said Julie.

"I can't do that. We've been here too long. We've got to get away, or—"

I heard a scuffling of feet, and then something bumped on the door of the smoke-house.

"Bill Avon! Bill Avon!" called Julie.

"Yes, Julie," said I.

"Ah-h-h!" said the girl.

"You see?" said Will Cary. "Now, come away, or there'll be the devil to pay. You don't know what a savage the old man is, up here. If he thinks—"

"Bill, are you all right?" asked Julie. "They haven't hurt you?"

"Not yet," said I, "but they may finish me before long."

"I'll get word to Charlotte," said Julie. "It's all because I made trouble that this happened. I'll never forgive myself. Bill, I'm sorry! I'm going to try—"

The voice of Will Cary struck in on her there, and I could hear him dragging her away, almost by force of hand.

Though the darkness, just after this, plugged up the chinks of fading daylights, I felt a good deal better. One friendly person in the world knew that I was locked up in that smoke-house, and, therefore, I could start building a few hopes. You may think that I was extravagant in my fears, but right up to that moment I had been expecting to find death just around the corner from me. You would understand if ever you could have seen the face and the eyes of the old man. But now I was a little comforted and lay out on the floor that was half sleeked down with grease and half roughed up with salt. I was hungry and thirsty, but the hope that was in me was better than a feather bed anywhere except in my own room at home.

Time takes on different meanings, when a fellow is locked up like that. A quick mind will live a day in an hour, and my mind was not slow when it came to building up apprehensions and making terrible pictures. Anyway, it was a good bit after the darkness closed in around the house before footfalls came, and the door was unlocked, and men came in with lanterns.

Several of them were Carys. I knew them by their hair, and their swarthiness, and their quick, bright eyes. But the most considered of the lot, the leader, was a tall fellow, almost as magnificiently made as Jim Silver, with rather a long, pale face, and long white hands, and a voice as deeply musical as I've ever heard. When he spoke, it was a sound that you wanted to listen to and dwell over. It was a voice that would never be forgotten. I never heard such manliness and gentle sweetness of tones joined together, and when I first heard him speak, I simply lost all fear of the place that I was in. I knew that no harm could ever come from a man with such a voice.

He was saying: "And that's Bill Avon? Poor fellow! I'm sorry to see him here. How are you, Bill?"

"I'm well enough," said I. I got up to my knees and then to my feet. "I'm well enough, but, of course, a smoke-house isn't a first-class hotel."

"Ah, no," said he. "No, it's not a first-class hotel."

He shook his head at me in a sort of sad sympathy.

"The trouble is that they want to know the plans you made with Jim Silver, and with Taxi, and that other man —Clonmel, they call him. They want to know what you planned with Silver and Taxi, most of all. Are they in the valley now?"

I wondered why the Carys had brought this man with the gentle voice to talk to me. He was probably a minister who knew something about the badness of the Carys, but who persisted in ministering to them because he would not save his care for the good people of his flock only. And the Carys, perhaps, had brought him in to see if he could persuade me to talk—before they had to use other methods.

"I can't talk about them," said I.

"Ah, can't you?" said that pale man. "Think it over again, Avon. These people are rough men. They intend to give you a good deal of pain, I'm afraid, unless you'll talk to them and say what you know!"

"I'd rather hang!" said I.

For I thought of that noble and calm figure, Jim Silver, and dying for a honorable cause seemed a very little matter, just then.

"He'd rather hang," said the tall man. "Ah, that's an idea that might be used then. Throw a rope over that central beam, will you? We might even smoke him a bit when we've got him hung up."

I was utterly amazed to hear soft, musical laughter flow out of the throat of the pale man. A rope was instantly flung over the main beam above. My hands were tied behind my back. The noose was pulled around my neck.

"D'you know what you're doing?" I shouted. "You can strangle me, but I won't talk. Are you going to murder me, you snakes?"

"He asks if you know what you're doin', Barry!" said one of the Carys, chuckling.

The name hammered against my brain.

"Barry?" I gasped. "Are you Barry Christian?"

For, of course, the thing came over me with a sweep. The man who would pay the price for Parade. The man who would give up his right hand, surely, to gain some hold upon Jim Silver. Of course, it was Barry Christian! I had heard him described before, only no description could do justice to the marvelous sweetness of his voice. Even that quality was turned against him, when I knew his name. That gentle voice and manner made him more perfectly the fiend, not the man.

In answer to my question, he smiled on me, more kindly than before. But that kindness always was a matter of the lips and the voice. The eyes, which I now stared into, showed the real soul of Barry Christian, and there was no more mercy in them than there would be in the heart of a wolf. A winter hunger for cruelty burned out at me. It sickened me. It made me faint.

Then the rope tightened with a jerk that lifted me to my toes. Three men were ready to give the haul that would dangle me in the air.

"If you twist your feet together and kick down with them," said Barry Christian, "I'll know that you're ready to talk. Pull him up, boys!"

I was already drawn up to my toes, yet there seemed to be the weight of a ton to be added to the rope as I was wrenched into the air. The noose sank into my throat until it seemed to grip the spinal column. You may think that hanging is like holding the breath under water. It is not. For an instant, I saw the peering, frightened and delighted faces of the Cary men. I saw the eyes of Barry Christian. And then a whirl of black agony took me. I twisted my feet together and kicked down.

I didn't realize that I had touched the floor, after that,

71

or when the rope was loosed. The next I knew, I was listening to the horrible, tearing sound of my own breathing. I was biting at the air, unable to get my lungs full of it.

Gradually I was able to see again. The face of Christian, quietly smiling, loomed greater than life-size. Then it receded to normal proportions, and I was able to see things as they were.

"Well?" said Barry Christian. "You'll talk now?"

"Yes," I gasped. "When Taxi and I found that Parade was gone, and the wolf dog, I went up to find Silver. Clonmel, of course, had located him before. We got together, all four of us. We wanted to find out if the horse was up here. We thought that Will Cary and his father might have brought it here. Taxi or Silver would be recognized. We thought that I might be able to get through and spot the horse, if it were here, and then get back and report."

"Where were you going to meet them?" asked Christian.

"Outside the valley," said I. "Down the trail there's a grove of big pines on one side, and some small spruce on the other side of the valley. They were to wait there for me."

"I know the place!" said one of the Cary outfit.

I could have thanked him with all my heart for remembering it. It seemed to give a body and a substance to the lie I had told. Christian stepped closer to me. His eyes hunted inside my mind, and something fled away within me, trying to escape like a hare followed by hounds.

"Well," he said, "it may be a lie, but I'll have to put up with it. Terribly sorry that I had to use such strong measures on you, Avon, but you know how it is. People like Barry Christian can't afford to waste much time. If, by any chance you've been lying and I find out about it—"

He wound up that speech with a snap of his fingers, and I knew that my life would end if the lie were spotted. That was the thought that remained with me when the door was shut and I was left in the thick darkness.

13 / Another Prisoner

I LAY THERE fingering my sore throat and staring with popping eyes at the blackness. I think I was almost more afraid of the fury that must be raging in Charlotte by this time, than I was afraid of Barry Christian and the Cary tribe.

Then I began to wonder about things—about the way Old Man Cary and Christian must appear when they were together, and which of the pair would take the lead, and which would have the most evil mind. I wondered about Julie Perigord, too. If she had had any doubts about Will Cary before she met Clonmel, what must those doubts be now? Or did she take this whole brutal clan for granted?

In the middle of that wondering, I fell soundly asleep. I wakened with an uproar, like a windstorm, working in my mind, and as my senses came slowly out of the house of sleep, I realized that it was not a wind at all, but the noise of many voices.

There was a gay, happy ring to them. Men were calling and shouting and laughing. They poured up to the smoke-house; a key jarred in the big steel lock, and then the door opened, and the staggering lantern light showed me the gigantic form of Harry Clonmel being thrust into the room.

The others came after him. I got up to my feet with difficulty, because they had left me with my hands still tied behind me. And in the steadying lantern light, I had a better view of Clonmel.

They had not taken him without a struggle. The clothes hung in tatters from him. Mud and blood were streaked across him. His whole right shoulder and half his chest were naked. Blood from a small tear in his neck gave out a wandering rivulet of crimson that made his skin whiter.

His feet were hobbled. His hands and elbows were tied behind his back. But he stood as straight and proud as though he were the conqueror and the others were beaten.

I never saw such a picture. He was big enough in body, but his spirit was so much larger still, that he overwhelmed me. He made me blink my eyes.

Barry Christian was there. His own clothes looked as ough he had been through a struggle. He was very cheerful, smiling, speaking in his gentle, soothing voice which I had come to detest. The poison of the man reeked in the very air, so long as my eyes were on him.

"So," said Christian to me, "you lied about it, did you? But the lies of old men are easily found out. I told you what would happen to you if the lie came to the surface. Well, you can pick out your own sort of trouble. There'll be plenty of it, my friend!"

I looked at him. I looked at that glorious figure, Clonmel, and suddenly—I don't know why—I wasn't afraid of death. My distrust and hatred for that fellow Christian choked out every other feeling.

"You dog!" said I to Christian, and the sound of my own voice amazed me.

He walked up to me and looked into my eyes. Nothing inside my soul ran away from him now. I was able to summon my strength and repel him and meet him half way, so to speak.

"Well, well," said Barry Christian. "No matter how old we are, it appears that we can always grow up!"

He chuckled, after he had said that, and turned to one of the others to ask where Old Man Cary was. They said he was coming. At that moment someone cried out in an agony, far away.

"They're settin' Luke's busted leg," said a voice.

"But when we get through with Clonmel, there ain't goin' to be nothin' left to set!" said another.

It was that lad Chuck. He sneaked up to Clonmel with his hand on the hilt of a knife.

"When we get through with you, you're goin' to be whittled right down to a boy's size. You hear?" he shouted at Clonmel.

He might as well have talked to a face of stone. Harry

74

Clonmel simply turned his head a little and shut that section of the scene out of his brain.

I wondered what had happened. Silver and Taxi had not been taken or killed. That was certain, or else I should have heard their names long before this. But there had been a glorious battle when they put their hands on Harry Clonmel.

I would have liked to have seen that. I wondered to myself if, when I saw such a thing, I would somehow find the courage to forget myself and jump into the war. And I felt a savage satisfaction that in the fight Clonmel had at least broken bones. He was ready to break more of them—neck bones, at that!

Then we could hear Old Man Cary coming. It was strange how quietly the Cary outfit stood, eying the monster, Clonmel. More than one of them had felt his hands. I saw one burly man with a bulge on his jaw as big as a fist, and others were marked. They stood quietly and looked at the man with hunger in their faces. They were like good fighting dogs eying a bear that has been partly baited and tied up again.

I heard Old Men Cary saying: "Watch how you walk. M'ria, you ain't as weak as all that. You can stiffen yourself a pile more. You ain't much more useful than a walkin' stick."

Then I saw the tall form coming up the steps and across the threshold with one arm stretched across the shoulders of the girl.

"Don't bring her in here," said Barry Christian sharply.

"No? And why not, Barry, my son?" asked Old Man Cary.

"Because a woman can't see things with the eyes of a man."

The old man laughed, and the sound seemed to be tearing and choking in his throat. The laughter made him look more like a boy than ever, and, therefore, more horrible.

"I raised her and I handled her," he said. "She ain't too much of a woman. Her eyes, they'll see things the way any Cary man would see 'em. Better'n most. Oh, a pile better'n most. Eh, M'ria?"

She did not answer. To hold her grandfather's arm over her shoulders, she gripped his skeleton fingers with one upraised, young, brown hand. She kept that grip, her shoulder against the bony chest of the old man to steady him on his feet, and in the meantime she looked deliberately about her. When she came to me, she dismissed me. When she came to Clonmel, her glance quietly followed the course of his blood. She smiled a little.

I think it was the most frightful thing I've ever seen, the smile of that girl as she looked at the running blood. It made me sick. It was monstrous.

"Well, let her stay," said Christian, at that.

"Oh, yes. We'll let her stay, all right," said the old man. "Now you got two chickens in your coop, what are you goin' to do with 'em, Barry, my son?"

"Wring their necks," said Barry Christian.

It didn't shock me to hear that. Somehow, after the smiling of the girl, murder was a very common idea. It was what was to be expected.

The old man took Maria over to face Clonmel. Old Cary reached out a skinny forefinger, all covered with the grime of the gun cleaning, and poked the ribs of Clonmel. He was in such perfect condition that with his breathing the strong bone frame showed through the outer layering of muscles. And the old man poked again at the swelling strength that covered the chest of Clonmel, and then jabbed his finger into the big round column of his throat.

"Ay, ay, ay!" said the old man. "Think of all the blood that's in him, Barry! I'm goin' to want to be on hand to see it sluice out of him. I'm goin' to feel younger, when I see the red come out of him, eh?"

He started shaking his head.

"I had to ask your opinion," said Barry Christian. "I suppose the best way is to take them down to the big creek and finish them there. The white water will chew them up so small that not even a button will be found later on."

"I've heard tell that the water will do that," said the old man. "Only, I was thinkin' is it wise to wring their necks so quick? Are they ripe for killin', Barry?"

"What do you mean by that?" asked Barry Christian. He turned to the old man, who said, still wagging his head:

"Kill 'em today, and where do you think Jim Silver and Taxi will be tomorrow?"

"I don't know. If they're anywhere near, we'll have a chance to run them down. Silver will never leave my trail till he's tried his chance to get Parade again—Parade and the gray wolf!"

True," said the old man, "but he ain't goin' to rush on account of horse blood. But on account of man blood— oh, he'll have to hurry on account of that!"

"Go on," said Christian impatiently. "Hurry?"

"Yeah. He'll hurry," said the old man. "You boys been tellin' me a lot about Jim Silver. You been tellin' me how brave and free and noble and good he is. Ain't you been tellin' me that?"

Christian took in a breath, with his mouth sneering. He said nothing. The old man went on:

"And a gent that's all those things which Silver is, how could he go and leave a coupla dear friends of his in our hands without makin' no effort?"

"He doesn't know that Avon is here," said Christian.

"But he knows that Clonmel is gone, or he will know, pretty soon. Unless our boys snag him up the creek, when he comes back to the place where you found Clonmel. He'll know what's happened, and he's sure goin' to start for us."

"He's not a fool," said Christian. "Even Jim Silver can't do any good for his friends here."

"A good man," said the grandfather, "ain't the kind to stop and think too long. A good man, Barry, is the sort that'll throw himself away for a lost cause. It's kind of noble, that is. A good man, he loves to be noble, I tell you. Silver's goin' to be noble. He'll come up here, sure enough, whether you think so or not. And we gotta keep the bait in the trap till he shows up!"

The detestable old devil began his husky laughter again, as he finished saying this.

Then Clonmel burst out: "You dirty rats! Silver won't come. Silver has a brain in his head. He'll never come, no matter how long you keep us. And if you leave me in here, I'll find a way out. I'll find a way out if I have to bite through the wood with my teeth!"

"Listen, listen!" murmured the old man, apparently in admiration. "Hear him talk, tryin' to persuade us to wring his neck *now*! Tryin' to persuade us to put the bait out of the trap so's Jim Silver can be kept out of it. And what might Jim Silver be to you, son?"

Why, when I heard that question, I wondered a little, myself. But when I glanced aside to Clonmel, I thought that I could understand. There was in the giant the sort of nobility that could feel all the majesty of a man like Silver; the sort of nobility that makes a few human beings willing to die for the right.

Yet, as I looked into the face of Clonmel and saw the tense expectancy and suffering in it, I felt that the old man was right. There was something very strange behind those lost words of the giant.

"I think you're right," said Christian suddenly. "We'll keep them."

"Of course, I'm right," said the old man. "I'm always right. I'm too near dead to enjoy bein' wrong any more."

14 / The Man of Action

I REMEMBERED THAT it was a long time after we were stifled by the blackness before I could speak, and then Clonmel asked me: "What happened?"

I told him briefly, and asked him how it had gone with him. He said that the three of them had waited for a long time, and finally Taxi had declared that I must have gone home, or perhaps even that I had sold my information to the Cary outfit, because Taxi said that money sometimes is a pretty strong voice in the ears of poor men.

"But Silver," said Clonmel, "swore that you would never back out of the job. He was as sure of that as he was

78

sure of anything in the world. He said, too, that it's the people who *have* money who will mostly sell themselves to get more of it. He's a wise fellow, that Jim Silver!"

Wise? I thought he was something more than wise. His faith in me made me strong. Another man's faith always multiplies one's own, I think. It seemed suddenly ridiculously easy to do the right thing without regret afterward.

I asked Clonmel what happened to him. He said:

"We'd waited a good while for you. It was after dark. Taxi and Silver talked over different things to do, and Silver suggested, finally, that you might have been caught up by the Carys. In that case, Taxi said, you were probably already dead, because the only law in this valley is what Old Man Cary pleases to give to everybody in the place.

"Silver said that you might have decided, after all, to go back and say good-by to your wife before you came over to the Cary Valley. He and Taxi went up to the head of the creek to see if they could spot you coming. They went off up the creek, and I stayed where I was, because it seemed to me a wild-goose chase. I walked up and down through a clearing at the side of the creek.

"That was where I was a fool. Silver had told me to keep my ears open and my eyes working. I should have done that, but I didn't. I walked around, and the rush of the creek was loud enough to drown out any quiet sounds, such as people on the prowl would make. The first thing I knew, a man told me to stick up my hands. There he was, standing beside a tree, as I turned around. I put up my hands, all right, but I put up a foot, too, and kicked him under the chin. The bone must have broken. I heard something snap, anyway.

"But as I turned to jump, three or four others piled onto me. We had a good brawl. They tapped me over the head enough times to make things hazy for me. Finally, they got me tie up, and they brought me on here."

I considered that talk, for a moment. That's the way a man of action expresses himself. There was no story in it. There was no dwelling on all the details. I wanted to know how he'd happened to break the leg of a man. I said:

"You smashed up one of them. How did that happen?"

"Well," said Clonmel, "In the middle of the brawl, they were all heaped up on me, and I managed to heave myself out of the pile. I caught a fellow by one leg and used him for a club. I swung him a couple of times and knocked them scattering. But the second time I used him, the club broke off short at the handle. I mean, the leg turned into pulp. That was all."

I closed my eyes and took in a breath. I was glad that grip had not fallen on my leg, for one thing, I can tell you!

I heard Clonmel say: "I'm going to get out of this. So are you. I'm not going to die in here. I'm not ready to be slaughtered in a meat-house like this."

I said nothing. There was nothing to say.

He came over to me and asked me what sort of cords had been used on my hands. I told him that cords had not been used, but rope that was almost half an inch thick.

"That's not thick enough, then," said he. "Twine might have held us, but not that pulpy stuff. Lie down flat on your face."

I did as he said, and he got down beside me and found the rope that bound my wrists together. He began to tear at the rope with his teeth. It put a shudder in me—the strength of his jaws and the strange feeling, as though a beast were at work. Sometimes, as he wrenched at the cords, the strength of his pull lifted almost my entire weight. And I could hear the popping sounds as he got his grip under strand after strand of the rope and parted it. It might have been half an hour before the rope actually parted.

I've told that to other people who would hardly believe it, but then not many of them had ever seen Clonmel. At any rate, there I was, with free hands, and though I didn't see what particular good free hands would do us, I found the knots that secured the ropes of Clonmel and undid them. That took only a few minutes more. He stood up, and I heard the swishing sound as he swung his arms.

"The roof!" he said to me. "If there's half a chance, I may be able to pry a log out of the roof."

I put myself against the wall, over in a corner, where I was sure that a beam ran overhead. Clonmel climbed on me. The bulk of him nearly smashed my bones, I can tell you, till he stood up on my shoulders and I heard him murmur that he had it.

Then he pulled himself up. After a time, I could hear faint, squeaking sounds.

Just over me his murmur said: "Come up here. Give me your hand and come up. The two of us may be able to wangle it!"

I found his hand, and his lifted me up easily. Yes, with the strength of one hand, he shifted my weight easily. I thought his grip was breaking the bones of my fingers. It was like the pressure of a mechanical device with the power of a machine behind it.

I climbed onto the rafter. He told me where to stand in the corner and what log to lift on, while he went down to the farther end of the beam and heaved at that section of the same log.

When he gave the signal, by hissing softly, I fell to work, but my efforts were not what put the shudder in the log my shoulder was against or the beam that was under my feet.

I might have guessed what followed, for, though that beam must have been at least three by four, it snapped suddenly at the farther and. I went down and rolled my length along the floor, and I heard big Clonmel bump not far away from me.

The door snapped open. Lights came in. Those fellows paid little attention to me. One man simply backed me into a corner with his gun, but five or six of them piled on Clonmel. Even then they had a terrific job of it until someone managed to slip the noose of a rope over his arms. After that they were able to hold him and lash him, while the noise of his breathing sounded like that of a bull. Right through the trampling, panting, and cursing, I could hear the labor of his lungs, while they rolled him in enough ropes to have compressed a bale of hay.

They tied me up again, too. Will Cary had charge of the entire job, and he did a good one, you can be sure.

When we were tied up, and when wires had been used to make sure what ropes apparently were not able to accomplish, Will Cary stood over Clonmel where the giant was stretched on the floor, unable to stir.

"I've got you—and I've got her!" said Will Cary.

I wondered, for a moment, what he was talking about, and then I heard Clonmel laugh.

"You haven't got her," he declared. "You haven't even got the ghost of her. She's seen the truth about you, Cary, and she smiles when she thinks about you!"

Cary pulled back his foot and kicked Clonmel in the face. I saw blood come to answer the blow, but Clonmel kept on laughing. Cary stood trembling and cursing over his man, for a moment, and then went out and ordered the others out ahead of him. When it came to the killing of Clonmel, at the will of the old man, I had an idea that Will Cary would have the ordering of it. If superior hate counted, he would certainly be selected for the job.

We could hear the voices muttering outside the smokehouse, now, and there was an occasional glinting of a lantern through one of the chinks as a guard walked up and down, carrying his light with him.

"I'm sorry," said Clonmel, "but better to have tried that than to be twiddling our thumbs. Talk to me, Bill. Talk to me about Will Cary. Fine, upstanding fellow to look at, isn't he?"

"As handsome as I ever saw, barring one," I answered. I did not tell him that the exception was himself. "I hated to see what he did to you, Harry."

Clonmel actually laughed again. What a man he was!

"I'm going to sing a little serenade for my girl. D'you think she cares a rap about me, Bill?"

"Cares about you? She's dizzy about you. But she's not for you, maybe."

"She's up here, I think," said Clonmel, "and if she is, she has to know that I'm out here."

He rolled over and put his mouth close to one of the chinks through which the lantern light glowed, now and again. Then he opened his throat and sang such a rollicking, thundering, ringing son as I'd never heard come out of a human being before.

A hand beat on the door of the smoke-house almost at once.

"Be still!" called Will Cary.

Clonmel kept on with his song until it ended. But by that time Cary had torn the door open and rushed in with his lantern in one hand and a gun in the other. He was a raging devil.

"I ought to empty the lantern on you and let you burn for a wick!" said Cary. "By thunder, I think I'll do it."

"Tell her that I was singing for her when you murdered me, Will," said Clonmel. "No, you won't have to tell her. She's heard me and the song both, by this time."

Cary swung up the lantern. I thought he would bring it down with a crash across the face of Clonmel, but instead he held his hand and stepped back. Whatever was in him for utterence, he could not get it past his lips, and he turned and walked slowly back through the open door. It slammed heavily behind him. The key ground in the lock, and I heard it rattle as it was withdrawn again.

"What possessed you?" I asked Clonmel.

"She had to know that I'm here," said Clonmel. "If she cares a rap about me, it'll keep her from mating with any Cary after I'm gone. Even if she doesn't care about me, she may ask a few questions that'll make them tell a few lies. And so, something of me lives after me."

I thought that over. There was a good deal in what he said, though his mind was not like the minds of others. I was still lying there, pondering him even more than I thought about our danger, when I thought I heard a very light, scratching sound, as though a cat were sharpening its claws against the wall outside. But this noise progressed steadily up the logs toward the roof.

15 / Guns in the Dark

AFTER A MOMENT, I rolled myself over toward Clonmel and whispered to him what I thought I heard. He agreed. He had heard the same thing. He pointed out that the sound now seemed to be coming forward along the roof.

"Is it Silver?" he murmured.

"I don't know," I said. "Unless he has more than one man to help him, what can he possibly manage to do here?"

"He doesn't doubt himself as much as you doubt him!" suggested Clonmel. "But they can't work up the logs of that roofing—not without crowbars and a lot of noise. What'll they do? They'll simply try the front door."

"While a man's walking up and down in front of it, on guard?" said I.

"That's all right," answered Clonmel, still in a whisper. "Jim Silver won't give up the ship, old son."

I could feel my pulse in my forehead and in my lips. There's nothing more exhausting then long fear, long expectation, and I felt as though my endurance had rubbed thin as a shingle, ready to break at a touch. I rolled over to the front wall and put my eye at the largest chink I could find between the floor and the edge of the wall.

I could see the guard pacing up and down. His lantern was hung on the side of a tree. The light of it stretched his shadow long or short along the ground.

He was a fellow I had not noticed before. He was close to forty, big and splendidly made, like all of the Carys, and wearing a short beard that was trimmed to a point. It was stiffly curling and such a glossy black that in certain lights it glistened like colored glass. The sheen of his eyes, under the deep brim of his hat, matched the gloss of his beard. He made a romantic figure, as he strode along there with a fine swing, but it wasn't his magnificence that impressed me. It was the rifle that he carried under his arm, and the pair of revolvers that weighted his cartridge belt. He had an air of authority. He had the air of one who would astonish himself if he missed a shot.

When he came to the end of his beat, though he was out of sight, I could hear him speak, each time. He said softly: "Hi!" or "Here!" as he turned to swing back past the front of the smoke-house once more. Now that I was listening for the sounds, with my ear close to the chink, I could hear dim answers, and I knew that other men were walking on at least two other sides of the building.

If those were friends of ours on the top of the house, how had they managed to climb there, unobserved? That was what baffled me. I gave up hope at once and decided that they could not be friends, but must be another pair of guards. It seemed that the Carys were ready to treat Jim Silver and Taxi as though they were a pair of hawks that were apt to drop down out of the sky!

That metaphor had just occurred to me when my bearded man came striding along about opposite the door. He stopped, looked up suddenly, so that I saw the strange white of his throat beneath the beard. And that was the moment that the blow struck him.

The object moved so fast that I could not tell what it was, for an instant. Then I saw the guard lying on the ground, and a big man rising from the prostrate form. That big man was Jim Silver!

My heart gave one great stroke, then all the blood in my body ran warmly and easily through the channels. For, if Silver was there, only a fool would stop hoping.

As Silver rose, the big guard threw up his hands. Silver leaned and struck him behind the ear. I heard the dull, clicking noise as though the knuckles sounded through the thin flesh against the bone of the skull. The guard turned limp. Silver straightened, and caught out of the air another form, softening the fall so that the man alighted noiselessly on the ground. That was Taxi, who sprang instantly out of my field of vision toward the door, while Silver scooped the hat of the fallen man off, jerked it over his own head, and caught the rifle up under his arm.

Then he in his turn stepped out of my line of sight, and a moment later I heard him say softly: "Hi!" at the next corner of the building.

At the same time, a light, scratching sound of metal against metal began in the lock of the door.

I could understand the idea then, though it was the sort of a thought that only the calmest brain in the world could have conceived in the beginning, or the steeliest nerves have attempted to execute. Somehow, the pair of them had managed to get up the rear of the smoke-house, and, working across the roof, Silver had dropped out of the air and had flattened the guard on duty there. Besides, he was to walk up and down and give a glimpse of himself at the alternate corners, repeating the single word each time, as the others were doing. And while he in this manner kept up the face of things, Taxi was to pick the lock and set us free.

I could remember more stories about Taxi now. It was said that, before he joined Silver, he had made his living by his mastery of that same art of picking locks. Well, I wished him millions of dollars' reward, no matter how he came by it, if only he could succeed in mastering the intricacies of that big steel lock which secured the smoke-house against thieves.

Just there, when my hopes were beginning to gallop like horses, I heard a voice from the rear of the cabin sing out loudly:

"Pete? Pete?"

"Hi?" called the guarded voice of Jim Silver.

"That you, Pete?" asked the other.

"Oh, the devil—" said Silver, not loudly, and again appeared to me, stepping calmly past the front of the cabin.

I waited, on edge, but there was no repetition of the question from the rear of the smoke-house. That casual answer had soothed the suspicions of the other guard, and I suppose the words were sufficiently natural to cover up any dissimilarity of voices. As a matter of fact, all bass voices have a faculty of sounding more or less alike.

Still the light, scratching sound continued at the door until I heard a heavier noise, though still very subdued, and then the door swayed open. A broad, truncated cone of lantern light appeared in the room, and showed me the broken beam on which I had stood with Clonmel.

Through that light slithered Taxi, with a winking bit of steel in his fingers.

He got to big Clonmel and freed him. I heard the slash of the sharp edge as it went through the ropes. He sprang to me, afterward. And I give you my word that his coming was as soundless as a shadow. An owl could not have moved more softly through the air. It seemed to be a bodiless thing that leaned over me, but it was no ghostly unreality—the fact that I was free, a moment later, from the grip of the ropes.

I got to my feet and swung my arms and flexed my knees to get the blood going and the sense back into my nerves.

Outside, I could hear Jim Silver saying: "Hi!" at a corner of the smoke-house, as he turned on his fake beat. Taxi, gripping me with one hand, and big Clonmel with the other, was saying in a whisper:

"Don't run, but walk. Walk straight out the door, past the trees, around the side of the smoke-house. Walk steadily. Jim and I will be behind you."

I led the way. I suppose it was hard for Clonmel to turn his face for flight before he had had a chance to get his grip on one of those rascals.

However, I could clearly feel and hear him striding behind me as we went out of the door of the smoke-house.

There were clouds in the sky, but there were stars, too, and the look of them was the finest thing that ever came to my eyes, I can promise you. And if I looked at the stars, the stars seemed to be looking right back at me!

I stepped past the motionless length of the bearded man, Pete. His arms were stretched straight out at his sides. His mouth was open, and he looked more dead than stunned.

I went beneath the big hood of the branches of the tree where the langern was hung, and then into the cone of shadow on the farther side of the tree. It certainly felt good to me, that shadow.

The big, sprawling house of the Carys was before me now. I went around the corner of it with Clonmel now stepping at my side. Indoors, we heard voices, and then a hearty burst of laughter startled me. It was oddly as though someone had been watching us all the time and now was deriding our silly little efforts to escape.

I had to think back with a start to Jim Silver. I had to remember that Jim Silver never did silly things.

Except, somehow, that he had let Clonmel take Parade and Frosty!

Then we were in front of the house, where a full dozen of saddled horses were tied to two long hitch racks.

A light football came up from behind me. That was Taxi, whispering:

"Take every horse. Tie the reins together. We've got to delay 'em, old man. Don't be rattled. Steady, old man!"

Steady? Yes, if I could make my fingers behave like flesh and blood instead of like frozen pieces of nerveless wood. But I began to untie the horses, one after another. One of them threw up his head suddenly, and theh rattling of the bridle made my heart jump. It seemed to me louder than the chiming of heavy church bells.

Then from the rear of the house came the thing that I was set for, that my whole soul was ready and opened by dread to perceive, so that the echoes of the noise ran through me and set all the nerves tingling like responsive wires. It was the short, heavy bark of a revolver!

I had four of the horses linked up. I got into the first saddle with one jump. A trained circus athlete could never have mounted faster. I pulled the head of the mustang around, and it seemed to me that it took a whole minute to get the iron-mouthed brute turned.

If only I had had spurs! Whereas I had only heels to grind into the ribs of the horse!

The sound of the gun had echoed through my soul; it had echoed through the house, too, and started doors banging and heavy feet bumping here and there. More gunshots followed, and then voices began to yell the alarm.

I tried to untangle the sounds in my memory and recall

what they were, but I can only remember one word, over and over again: "Silver! Silver! Silver!"

Well, if the old man had not known Silver before, he would know him after this!

Then a tall form came around the corner of the building and leaped into a saddle with a fantastic bound. That was Jim Silver. And with the sweep of the whole procession of horses, we plunged away.

Two more figures came flickering around the corner of the house. They were shooting as they ran. One of our horses reared and squealed. I saw Silver shoot, and one of the shadowy forms spilled along the ground.

He fired again. The second went staggering.

The door of the house opened behind us, letting out a rush of light and of voices, but now we were tearing at full speed through the dark shelter of the trees.

16 / The Pursuit

REVOLVERS ARE bad business inside a house or at short range, but there's nothing so infernally convincing as the ringing explosion of a rifle at a little distance, and the way the rifle bullets went cracking through the branches kept me flattened along the neck of the mustang.

We came out into the open, beyond the trees. The long, dry grass swished like water around the legs of the horses, and the beat of the hoofs was so muffled that far away we could hear the squealing of half-wild broncos as the Carys caught up fresh mounts and threw saddles on them.

We had a good lead, but not a secure one, for we knew that the Carys would get out of their horses all that savage Indians could get. That was what they were—Indians. And they had the blood thirst high in their throats.

Beyond the trees, I saw that a moon was rising, the big yellow circle just detaching itself from the hills. We were aimed right at it, and I remember that the light seemed to make a path over the flat of the ground, like a light's path on water. It was all very beautiful, but when that same moon was a little higher, it would furnish excellent light for the rifles of the Cary clan.

Silver swung over toward me.

"Avon," he said, "you know this country better than any of the rest of us, it seems. What's the best way out?"

"The way we came in," said I.

"We can't go that way. It takes us right back past the Cary house."

That was true. I looked rather wildly around me. It upset me to have to lead the way, even as a guide, because such men as Taxi and Silver ought to be ruling all of our movements. Besides, I really knew very little about the valley, except two or three times, on long hunting expeditions, I had come to the verge of the cliffs and looked over that forbidden land. The high wall of stone was broken in only a few places, where creeks, large or small, had eaten through the barrier, but all of the creeks had not cut out valleys that were passable; some of the waters had dropped down through box canyons that even a mountain sheep could not wander through.

I looked along a glint of water ahead of us and saw by glimpses of brightness that it wound away toward a black, yawning mouth in the wall of the cliffs. Certainly that opened a good promise, and I pointed it out.

"That ought to be the next best way," I called to Silver.

He nodded in answer and turned his horse in that direction. We made time as fast as we could hoof it along, because the great object, of course, was to get out of sight before the Cary horsemen swarmed out on our trail; as I forced my bronco into a racing gallop, I kept looking back over my shoulder. The plain behind me was dark, because I was looking away from the moon, and the trees that screened the Cary house were like big storm clouds. Riders out of those clouds would be like lightning flashes to me, not matter how dimly they appeared.

But we pulled up to the mouth of the canyon without seeing a single pursuer. It was only as I kicked my mustang through the gap that it seemed to me something came out from the trees. It was like seeing shadows of shadows, but I knew it was real. That flick of a glimpse, that mere hint, was composed of riders on running horses. I could hope, however, that they hadn't seen us, for the shadows of the rocks fell down on us, thrown by the rising moon.

In the meantime, we poured through that canyon, and rounding a sharp elbow bend, we came smash on the end of our way. There was a big cliff of hard stone—granite, perhaps. It was glistening white with the moon above, and ink-black with shadow below, and the little wan brightness of the falling water streaked a glimmer of reflected moonshine down through the shadow. It was a whale of a cliff. It was a good hundred feet high, and instead of offering foothold, here and there, it actually swayed back from the top toward the base. A lizard would have grown dizzy looking at the thing, to say nothing of trying to climb it. And like measuring sticks to show up the height of the stone, there were some tall, slender trees, straight-shafted and arrow-tipped, that stood up from the floor of the valley.

We stopped our horses and looked around us. We could hear the panting of the horses, the saddle leather creaking a good deal as the mustangs heaved their sides. And I could hear the unspoken words of the men who were condemning me for pointing out a blank trail.

Then we swung around and hurried back to the mouth of the shallow little box canyon.

It was a whole lot too late to do anything in that direction, for the moon was brightening all this while and shaking silver dust over the grass of the plain. And in the middle of the plain came the men of the Cary clan.

They looked more terrible to me than wild Indians. Wild as Indians they were, and more cruel, and more formidable in wits. And the numbers of them! There was a cluster of twelve or fifteen at the head of the search, and others kept ripping out of the woods with whoops. Even at that distance, I could hear the thin yells walking across the air of the night. A fine sight, a stirring picture— to be looked at in a book!

I glanced aside at Jim Silver, sitting very still on his

horse, with a hand on his hip. The moon fell full on his face, so that I could see the tranquillity of it, and I knew the meaning of the phrase "ready to die." He was ready. He must always have been ready. Perhaps that was why he had rubbed shoulders with death so many times and escaped. But most of the time he had had with him a horse that nothing could match, or that wise devil of a Frosty. Now he was stripped of his tools—and Clonmel had stripped him.

It would not have been strange, when he saw how we were bottled up, when he saw that we could not venture out of our hole in the ground without being rushed by the hunters, if he had turned and cursed Clonmel heartily. Instead, I saw him put out his hand casually and drop it on the huge shoulder of that tattered figure. I heard Clonmel say in a choking voice: "Jim—" And Silver answered gentle: "Hush, old son!"

There was something between the pair of them, something that would make Silver give more than horse or wolf, or even life, to this young giant.

"They're working the trail with Frosty. They'll soon be here," said Silver, after that.

I had not seen at first, but now I could make it out. I could see the figure of the big lobo on the end of the lariat, straining forward across the plain, and the riders cantering easily after him. They had brought out Frosty, knowing that he would follow the trail of his master with a perfect certainty. A horrible thought, it seemed to me, that the love of the beast for the man should have been used to kill Silver. And that was what they meant. The rest of us didn't count. Not even Taxi, not even the hugeness of Clonmel counted. Jim Silver was the man they wanted. If they got him, Barry Christian would flood their wallets with hard cash. Barry Christian himself, with that invincible enemy removed, would go on to build up for himself a new and greater empire of crime.

I could see one rider far loftier than the others, on a gleaming horse. That was Barry Christian, I had no doubt, on the silken brightness of Parade. And the whole current of fighting men was set directly toward us.

Silver said: "We'd better pull back from this."

Taxi broke out: "We can slip out and ride along the cliffs and, if they see us, we can make a running fight of it."

Silver simple said: "That won't do."

He didn't advance any arguments, and no arguments were needed. Cary rifles would not miss, even by moonlight, and all of us knew it.

Silver dismounted. We all did the same. He told me to take the horses back up the canyon. I did that and tethered them to trees. Then I hurried back.

We all had rifles from saddle holsters of the Cary clan. We had plenty of ammunition. If it came to a matter of siege, we could eat horseflesh and cut down trees to make fires, and there was water flowing through the ravine. But before long the Carys would be on the heights above us, as well as plugging the mouth of the ravine, and they would pick us off at their leisure. It seemed improbable that they would be able to scale the cliffs on either side of the ravine directly, but they could send back a party through the mountains, to come down from the headwaters of the little creek, and get at us in that way. I thought that out as I stood there, and saw the others ready with their guns.

Silver said: "I don't think there's any purpose in murdering them. There's only need to shoot one shot to turn them away from a charge."

"Murder?" broke out Clonmel. "Man, it wouldn't be murder—just plain justice!"

"There's only one Cary out there who deserves killing, probably," said Silver, "and that man is too old to be shot. He's trained the others up to be what we've found them. We might butcher half a dozen of them as they come on but I won't have it."

I could see the point of it. We couldn't kill enough of them to clear our path; the death of a few would simply make the rest more savagely bent on ending our lives. But more than these practical reasons, Silver would not shed blood without a more bitter necessity than this. I felt a cold sense of awe as I looked at him. There was no one like him. There would never be another cut out of the same metal. His ascendancy over us was so complete that there was no argument about it, whatever.

He was to fire one shot, and I wondered how he would direct it. I saw the sweep of the coming horsemen. We gathered in the thick of the shadow that slanted across the throat of the valley. Silver stood at wait, his rifle ready.

The riders were so close that I could make them all out—Christian riding at the front, and a man I couldn't name beside him. Yes, I *could* name him. It was Pete, who had stood guard and who had been knocked silly by Silver earlier in the night. He was the one who had Frosty on the lariat, holding the rope in one hand, with a loop of the slack around his arm.

I distinctly heard Silver mutter: "I'm sorry!"

Then he brought the butt of the rifle into the hollow of shoulder and, the instant it settled there, fired. It was as casual a shot as though he had been firing at a stump, but it made Pete's mustang pitch on its nose. Pete himself sailed through the air in a clumsy spread-eagle. He lighted, rolled, actually came to his feet, staggering straight on toward us, though the rest of the cavalcade had split to this side and that, running for cover.

Frosty, in the meantime, had leaped on ahead and had come to the end of the rope. One lunge more untwisted the rope from the arm of Pete. Frosty came to his master's whistle so fast that the rope stood out in the air in a straight line behind him. And Pete, swerving, sprinted for shelter.

Clonmel jerked up his rifle to fire. Silver struck it down again.

"No murder!" he said.

That was the only reason the Carys were able to bottle us up without spending human blood.

17 / Cary's Offer

NOW THAT WE WERE safely bottled up—of course the Carys knew that they had us—the yelling of those devil ran chills through me, and fevers, too. I could hear them laughing and shouting. They began to howl filthy insults at us. They were ready to run amuck with the sense of power. They had helpless things to handle now, and they wanted to get at the work of torment.

But after a time, I heard a voice calling out: "Hey, Silver! Hey, Jim Silver!"

Silver answered instantly.

Said the other: "The old man wants to talk to you. Can he come in?"

"Why not?" asked Silver.

"You gotta give your word that nothin' is goin' to happen to him or the gal with him."

"All right. I'll give you my word," said Silver.

"All right, Grandpa. You can go in!" shouted the voice.

It staggered me, that. I mean for those savages to be willing to take the word of Jim Silver at a time like that! It might be that the old man had not known about Silver the day before, but he certainly had had a chance to learn more about his character in the meantime.

We would not have trusted the Bible oaths of the whole gang, but they were ready to risk their lives if Silver gave his casual word! In a sense, I've always through that that was the finest tribute that any man could have received.

A little after this, Old Man Cary came into view, riding along with his long legs dangling down on either side of the little mule that carried him. He looked a good deal bigger than the mule. Half a length behind him was Maria on a mustang as pretty as a deer and just as wild.

95

It minced and danced and curvetted in great style, and she sat it out like an old-timer.

When Old Man Cary was well inside the mouth of the valley, he saw us and held up his hand, pushing the flat of it forward, like an Indian.

"How!" said he.

"How are you, Chief?" asked Silver calmly.

The old villain slid down from his mule. He was strong enough in the riding muscles to keep his place in a saddle, but he was not so sure when he stood on the ground again. The girl frisked off the back of her pony, threw its reins, and slipped under the extended, limp arm of her grandfather.

I hardly ever had had a chance to see her except in these attitudes of filial devotion, but I never suspected her of any special love for Old Man Cary. I dare say that her father and her mother were glad to have her near the old devil, because he probably handed out choice presents in the way of lands and opportunities to the couple on account of Maria, but the girl herself simply accepted the job and did it skilfully, calmly, like a doctor. While she supported the arm of her grandfather over her shoulders, her head kept turning, her bright eyes kept glinting at us, one after the other, until the gaze landed on Clonmel. That was enough for her. She ate him up steadily.

I must say that he was a picture to fill the eye of any barbarian, by this time. He had washed himself in the cold water of the creek, and had then thrown a slicker over his shoulders, and it looked like an Indian blanket. If Indians ever had white skins, he could have stood for the perfect picture of one of them. He looked thewed and sinewed and handed for anything.

The old man pointed to a flat-topped rock. The girl helped him to it and fetched out his pipe for him and filled it. She put the string-wound bit of the stem between his toothless gums and lighted a match and held it for him. He puffed a minute and then he said:

"Kind of comforts a man, tobacco does. You—you're Jim Silver?"

Silver was the one he had picked out and he kept pointing his scrawny arm, till Silver said:

"Yes, my name is Jim Silver."

"Your name ain't Jim Silver, but that's what you're called," said the old man.

"You can put it that way," said Silver.

He came up and sat on a rock, facing the chief of the Cary clan, the one man of the lot, he had said, who deserved killing.

The point came to that right away.

"Why didn't you boys plaster some of us when we was comin' up?" asked Cary.

"I haven't a grudge against the rest of them," said Silver. "They only do what they've been taught to do."

The old man cackled in his husky voice. Then he said: "That means me?"

"That means you," said Silver.

"Appears to me," went on Cary, "that you're kind of a biggish sort of a man, Silver. The kind that I used to do business with out here in the old days. The race of them has died out. I'm the only one left, pretty near. Biggish men. Not the pounds. That wasn't what counted. Nerve. They all had nerve! They was all nerve! Nerve and brains, like you and me."

It didn't seem to bother Silver, to be classed like that along with Cary.

"You've come here to say something," said Silver. "Why not say it? You fellows keep an eye around you. Watch the top of the rocks," he said to us.

"Oh, naw, naw, naw!" said Cary. "There ain't any trick about this here. I don't aim to get my gullet sliced open by talking to you boys till my gang gets into place for shootin'. M'ria, come back here!"

Maria had walked straight up to Clonmel and was talking to him, her body swaying back a little as she tilted he head to face him.

"I'll come when you need me," she said, without turning. And her voice began to run on, very softly, as she talked to Clonmel.

The old man was not angry. He merely chuckled, and there was that tearing sound in the bottom of his throat.

"She's seen a man for herself, and she's goin' prospectin' for him," said Cary. "Gals is like that."

He puffed at his pipe, smacking his loose lips loudly.

"Now I wanta make a deal with you, Silver," he said. "We got all the four of you, and we got you good. But the facts is that we don't wanta waste all the time we need for roundin' you up, and climbin' the mountains, and shootin' you down. We got all the four of you, but blottin' out one. It's four thousand times worse. One of you gents has got a wife and a ranch behind him. People raise hell when a rancher is wiped out. I dunno why. They ain't no better than nobody else. But posses is raised, and the State militia is called out on jobs like that. So what I mean to say is that while we got the four of you, good and proper, the only one we aim to collect is you, Silver. You walk out of here with me, and the rest of 'em can go free."

"Christian wants me rather badly, eh?" said Silver calmly.

"He right well hankers after you," said the old man. "I recollect once I was out in the mountains froze near to death above timber line and a storm raisin' the devil in the sky, and me in a cave freezin' and starvin' for three days, and the best that I could do was wait for that storm to blow over. And I got to thinkin', along toward the end of the second day, and what I thought about was corn fritters. And doggone my heart, Silver, if I didn't hanker after 'em so bad that I pretty nigh walked out into the storm, that third day. And I'll tell you what— Christian, he hankers after you the way I hankered after them corn fritters."

Silver turned a little.

"Bill Avon is the man to answer you. Shall I walk out with him, Bill?"

I would like to say that I answered right up, that I shouted it, and that I cried out that I would rather die than see Jim Silver done in on account of the rest of us. But the fact is that for a second I thought about the shack on the ranch, and the smell of the coffee in the kitchen, and the sound of Charlotte singing quietly over her sewing, and the way the taste of coffee and tobacco mixes in the mouth.

I came to with a gasp and said: "No, no, Jim! We stand together. You can't go."

"I'm sorry I asked you," said Silver.

"Hey, wait a minute and ask the others," said the old man.

"I don't need to ask them. I know them well enough to leave the question out," said Silver. "I could have answered for Bill, too, except as a matter of form." I was glad he said that.

"You take a lot on yourself," said Old Man Cary. "Are you scared to come?" he asked curiously.

He tilted his evil old head to one side and stared at Silver.

"Men aren't made of the stuff you think," answered Silver. "You've raised a lot of beef up here, partly on four feet and partly on two. You call them men, but they're not. They're a worthless lot, Cary, and you shouldn't judge other men by them. These fellows I'm with would rather lose their blood than have me walk out with you."

"Now, what the devil do you mean by all that?" asked Cary.

He was frankly bewildered.

"Why, I mean that the job can be bigger than the men in it," said Silver.

"I don't understand," said Cary.

"I didn't think that you would," said Silver. "But we're doing something together, not one by one."

"And that means?"

"It means that it's time for you to go back."

The old man stood up.

"Come here, M'ria," he called.

She came back to him slowly, her head turned a little toward Clonmel. Obediently she helped her grandfather to straighten. Then he exclaimed:

"The rest of you heard him talk. Ain't he talkin' through his hat? If he walks out, I'll tell you what, there ain't a hair on the heads of the rest of you that would be hurt."

Taxi laughed a little. He said: "Will you swear that, Cary?"

"Yes, sir. Sacred word of honor and cross my heart if I don't swear it."

"Honor?" said Taxi. "Cary honor?" He laughed again.

"Well, sir, I'll be doggoned!" murmured the old man. "You boys not having opened up and socked lead into us, I sort of figgered that there was need of talk between us. But I reckon I was wrong."

He turned his back and laid hold on the mule's withers and the cantle of the saddle.

"Have a hand?" asked Silver suddenly, seeing that the girl made no gesture to help the old man.

"Keep off!" snarled Cary. "When I can't climb a hoss on my own hands and feet, I'm goin' to be ready to plant."

He had to struggle with all his might, nevertheless. Half-way up, his whole body was shaking, and I thought his left foot would tremble out of the stirrup. But he made it, falling breathlessly and gasping, forward into the saddle.

He erected himself, after that, with the strength of his arms.

"See you later, boys," he said. "I'll see *all* of you later on."

18 / A Chance

I'M ASHAMED TO CONFESS that I felt pretty blue as I watched the backs of that pair go out of the mouth of the ravine and turn from view behind the rock. Silver said to me:

"Thanks, Bill."

"Jim," I answered him, "don't thank me. I'm sorry that I seemed to hesitate!"

"Tut, tut!" said Silver. "You couldn't do the wrong thing. I know that!"

Why, I can't tell you how that warmed my heart! No man can believe entirely in himself. That's the greatest value of friends. That's why their belief makes us better than we are, and that's why enemies make us worse.

I had just registered that idea in my brain, when Clonmel said:

"There's some way of doing something. I can't stand here like an ox and wait for the ax."

"You'll probably have to, though," answered Silver.

Clonmel did a strange thing. He threw back his head and made a two-handed gesture.

"Anyway, we'll be together, Jim."

"Aye, we'll be that," said Silver. But there was bitterness in his voice.

Almost more than freedom and safety, I wished then that I could know what lay behind those two. Silver sat there on the rock with Frosty lying across his feet, his head, free from the muzzle at last, raised and turned a little so that he could constantly watch the face and the gestures of his master. I noticed that when Frosty was with him, Silver rarely moved a hand, and the reason was, I dare say, that those movements were apt to have particular meanings for the wolf. There was a peculiar and complicated language that had developed between the pair of them. The lifting of a finger could make Frosty jump and run.

You've seen find hunting dogs work difficult country directed in and out and back and forth by the gestures of the hunter, and those dogs are generally trained in a few weeks or months, and given practice only a small number of hours each year. So when you can consider what might happen when an animal with a brain like Frosty's lived every hour of every day with a master whose companion he was on life trails and death trails, it was no wonder that word of voice or word of hand had instant meanings to the great brute.

With his return, Silver had half of his usual pair of companions, and I knew that his mind was constantly turning to the other half. I knew he was being tormented almost more by concern on account of Parade than by concern on account of himself. If he died, Barry Christian would ride the golden chestnut. The thought must be eating Silver's heart.

Another thing that I noticed was that Silver and Taxi rarely spoke to one another, but even by moonlight it was possible to see the expression change and soften when their glances crossed at any moment. They didn't need to talk to one another. They had been through too much together.

We had fallen into a silence, while the wind began to whisper secretly through the long, dry grass that covered the ravine. The tops of the slender trees swayed a little in the breeze. And always the moon was climbing, shrinking the shadows, brightening the center of the sky until the stars dwindled away.

Into that quiet a rifle report smacked against my ears like the flat of a slapping hand. I heard the whir of the bullet; I saw Silver spring sidewise to his feet, with Frosty bristling, on guard before his master; but it was Taxi who turned the trick.

At the sound of the gun, he had an automatic in his hand and he fired a burst of three or four shots in rapid succession. It was such rapid work that I couldn't see, easily, whether he was shooting high or low. But then I heard a clattering high up the cliff, toward the mouth of the ravine and on the right-hand side of it. I saw a rifle sliding down the rock, slithering here and there, then arching out from the cliff and falling sheer down until it smashed on the stones below. I thought I had an impression of a figure dropping behind the parapet of rocks up there, but I wasn't sure.

We got to cover in an instant, and as I stretched out behind a boulder with a feeling that death was already chilling me for the grave, we heard a wailing voice cry, beyond the valley:

"Chuck! Chuck! Are you there?"

"I'm here!" shrilled the answering voice of Chuck. "I missed; they winged me."

"Can you come down?"

"They're watchin' the place now. I can't come down."

That was true. I could see now what the daring young rat had done. He had sneaked in through the mouth of the ravine, edging along the ground, I suppose, and then he had managed to climb up along a series of crevices to the top. Any one of us could do the same thing, but we would be exposed to the guns of the men outside the valley. However, it was a good example.

"Are you bleedin' much, Chuck?" yelled the voice outside the valley.

"Naw, I got it stopped!" shouted Chuck. "I'm all right. I can see 'em down there. I scared hell out of 'em, too. I can see every jump they make, while I'm up here."

"Good kid. Stay there and watch 'em! Got a revolver?"

"No. And my rifle dropped when they plugged me."

There was a yell of anger from outside the valley.

Silver stood up from the shelter he had taken. If Chuck lied, bullets might begin to fly at us again, but apparently he had told the truth. There were no more shots from the top of the rock. We were safe again for a little while, at least, until those restless devils of Cary's managed to think out some new ways of plaguing us.

Silver and Taxi went the round of the ravine, looking for crevices similar to those which had enabled Chuck to climb to his crow's nest. They came back after a time and reported no luck.

Silver said: "But we've found one good chance for climbing out of this place."

"What chance did we find?" asked Taxi curiously.

"Those trees—some of them are near the edge of the cliff," said Silver.

"Use one of 'em for a ladder?" I asked.

"Yes," said Silver.

"That would be all right if we could chop one of 'em down," said Clonmel, "and lean it against the rock."

"There's not even a hand ax in the lot of us," said Taxi. "And who can jump thirty feet from a standing start?"

"We could girdle the easiest tree with fire and burn it down," I suggested.

"That would take hours," said Silver, "and we haven't hours. We may not have more than a few minutes before the Carys have another set of riflemen up there on the edge of the cliffs. They've been marching up through the hills—you can depend on it—ever since we came in here."

"No way of chopping the tree down," said Clonmel.

"No way of burning it down in time—then how *can* you make a ladder of it, Jim?"

"We'll try another dodge," said Silver. "Bill, are you good with a rope?"

I hesitated.

"Not the way you people are good with horses or guns —or wolves!" said I.

"You can daub a rope on a cow, and that's all I want. Look back there at that tree. Not the tallest one, but the one that's nearest the edge of the cliff. You see that one?"

I could see it, and nodded.

"Take a rope off one of the saddles and climb up there. Better take two ropes, while you're about it. When you get close to the top of the tree, try to noose the rope over one of the projections of rock that stick up above the edge of the cliff. Then pull in and see how close that will swing the top of the tree to the cliff."

There it was!

It was not salvation or us, exactly, but it was a hope of salvation. I stared at Jim Silver for one instant and wondered how that man *ever* could be really cornered by bad luck or the hatred of his enemies. His brain was too cool and his eye too quick to miss openings. And here, where I would have sworn that nothing could be done, he was already giving us our chance!

I got the ropes, went to the tree, and started climbing. And as I climbed, I could hear the shrill voice of Chuck informing his friends outside the ravine about my progress.

"Avon's got a pair of ropes. He's noosed them around his neck. Maybe the fool's goin' to hang himself. Now he's climbin' a tree. And now he's up close to the top. Now he's swingin' his rope. Now he's daubed it onto a rock. He hauls in tight and hard. The top of the tree swings in. He's goin' to make that tree into a ladder to the top of the cliff! He's goin' to give 'em a way out! Crowd in! Crowd in! Get ready to make a rush!"

I thought, in fact, that the trick was as good as done. I had hauled the rope in, hand over hand, and the tree was bending far over with my weight and the strength of my pull, when the narrow trunk of the evergreen—there must have been a deep flaw in the wood—cracked off right under my feet. I found myself entangled in the foliage, hanging onto the rope for grim life, and shooting forward through the air.

The whole treetop was swinging in with me, and that was what made the cushion when I crashed against the cliff. Otherwise, every bone in my body would have cracked, because the swing inward was a full twenty feet, I should say. As it was, I bumped hard enough to knock the wind out of me.

A lucky thing, then, that I had two lariats instead of one, because that gave me a rope line nearly eighty feet, and that was enough. I had a ten-foot fall from the end of the line, at that, but Silver and the others piled some brush together, and that was a safe mattress to drop into.

As I picked myself up, I could hear Chuck shouting the news from the bird's nest. He was happy about it, the young scoundrel. He was yelling that I'd smashed up —no, that I was on my feet, but that I was just about finished—that the tree business was finished for good and all.

Well, as I stood there, rubbing my rope-burned hands together, I was pretty willing to give up any idea of tree ladders.

But the next moment Chuck yipped out some information that brought all four of us to life.

"Will is comin'!" he shouted. "I can see Will Cary comin'!"

I looked far up toward the crest of the ravine, away above us, and there was enough moonlight to show me figures, or what might be figures, a mile or two miles away, stirring vaguely against the sky as they climbed down over an edge of rock.

19 / The Second Attempt

It seemed to me suddenly that young Chuck, up there in his post of vantage, was like an announcer, telling a crowd what fighters were entering the bull ring, and we were the bulls penned in the center.

I looked at Silver. Clonmel and Taxi were looking at him too. He simply said:

"There's another tree, almost as close to the cliff. Try that one, Bill."

Taxi got me the ropes. I went up that tree in a furious burst of effort. The yelling of the Cary tribe outside the ravine affected me more than applause. I climbed as though a panther were after me, reaching up with its claws every moment to drag me down. Because it was plain that if we could not get to the cliff before Will Cary and his party arrived there, we were finished utterly.

This tree was heavier and sturdier in every way than the first one I had tried. There was no chance of its breaking off under me, but for the same reason it would be harder to pull the head of it in toward the rock; besides, it was farther from the stone wall. However, I got the noose of the first rope over a projecting stone and hauled away. Then big Clonmel came up and called to me to throw the second rope. I did that, and passed the end of it down to him. In that way we hauled in till the head of the tree was inclined well over. We could see then that the farther we hauled, the more we could bring down the level of the ropes below the edge of the cliff. There was an eight-foot gap remaining that we would have to hand ourselves across.

And how were we to get across that gap, all of us, while Chuck was posted up high, ready to tell his family the instant we were off the ground and all committed to the tree? Why, the Carys would pour into the ravine and pick us off the tree like so many crows!

I could hear Chuck shouting: "They're goin' up the tree. Get ready, all of you! The minute they're all off the ground, I'll give you the word. You can give 'em hell!"

Of course, they could give us hell! As I tied the end of my rope around the tree, I looked vaguely about me. The voice of Silver came strongly up to us:

"Harry, hand yourself across the ropes to the rock. Bill, you follow him. Harry will give you a lift on the other side."

"I'll stay here till you come," answered Clonmel's shout.

"I'm coming right away," cried Silver. "Taxi, light the grass on that side of the creek."

Still I could not understand the idea, until I saw Taxi on one side of the creek and Silver on the other, kindling the grass here and there. Then it was clear. The wind that blew was passing down the canyon, and it ought to sweep a wall of fire through the valley. Behind that fire and smoke, which would hold out the Cary clan, we could all get up to safety, perhaps. All except Frosty! I wondered if Silver would kill the wolf rather than let him fall into the hands of the Cary outfit again.

Then I heard Chuck yelling out the news that the grass in the valley was being lighted. But already the crackling sound of the fire was enough to warn the Carys. The tall, dry grass seemed to be drenched with oil, it picked up the flames so fast. There was a running wall of fire in no time, with the smoke flowing back above the flames, outdistanced by them. And outside the valley, I could hear the Carys howling like angry devils.

I had something close at hand to pay attention to now. That was Clonmel, who was handing himself across the ropes, pulling himself along with powerful arm hauls. The whole tree staggered and shook with the violence of his efforts. He reached the farther side of the ropes, gave his immense body one pendulous swing, and thereon he was established on the safe shore!

It meant that we had an advance guard established; it meant that we had a fighting force ready to shelter the rest of our retreat, and for the first time a very real hope came up in me. I was glad to hear the voice of Chuck shrilling:

"Clonmel's across! He's on the rock. Bill Avon is throwin' the rifles across to him. They're all goin' to get free except the wolf! They'll get loose, unless you do something! Hey, Pete, Tom, Walt—crowd in and take a chance, or they'll get away!"

I had tossed the two rifles into the hands of Clonmel, by that time, and now I swung out on the ropes in my turn. It was ticklish work. The drop below me was enough to smash me to bits. I didn't dare to look down. And every time I loosened the grip of one hand and slid it forward along the rope, I felt sure that the hold of the other hand was slipping away!

Clonmel kept shouting encouragement to me. My arms began to shake, and my whole body was shuddering with fear. A rush of heat and smoke burst up around me, carried by a backwash of the air currents. Little glowing sparks and flaming grasses showered against my face and scorched it. I drew in a breath of hot smoke and gas that almost stifled me. I stopped moving; I stopped struggling.

The voice of Clonmel thundered through the fiery mist: "Come on, you weak-kneed quitter! Come on, you yellow coward!"

Somehow that abuse gave me new strength. It gave me anger in the place of fear, and I struggled forward. The great arm of Clonmel swept out over me like a crane. His grip fastened in my collar, and he dragged me lightly up over the edge of the rock.

I sat there, gasping, reaching for my rifle and getting ready to fight in the battle I was sure must come.

I saw the fire running like yellow horses with smoking manes down the length of the ravine. I heard the shouting of the Carys outside the valley and the wild voice of Chuck urging them to close in—to get into the creek and wade up the water, where the fire could do them no harm.

Well, I had not thought of that. They could come up the creek, of course, though it might be rather unpleasant work ducking between flame and smoke and water; elements in none of which a man could breathe.

Taxi slid out of the top of the tree and came across

the ropes like a wildcat. He was as light as a feather—the most active man I've ever seen.

When Taxi was beside the two of us, I noticed that Silver was no longer on the ground but that he was climbing, slowly and painfully, and there was no sight of Frosty on the ground. Then, as Silver neared the top of the tree, I had a good look at him, and made out that he was carrying Frosty on his shoulders!

It stopped my heart, somehow, to see that.

They came into plain view at the end of the ropes, and I saw Frosty embracing the neck of his master with his forepaws, exactly like a trusting child!

I don't suppose it was so wonderful. A thousand animals have done harder tricks than that. But just then it seemed to me that the soul of a human being must be inclosed within the pelt of Frosty.

But when they came to the ropes, how was that burden to be taken across?

Mind you, Frosty weighed a full hundred and fifty pounds.

But Silver had thought the thing out on his way up the tree. He got out under the ropes, hanging by his heels and his hands, and with a word to Frosty, he made the big animal crawl painfully out into the cradle that was furnished for him in this fashion.

Precarious? I wouldn't have done it for any human being, let alone for any animal. But then, for that matter, I haven't the strength to do such things.

Silver started hitching himself forward. I saw Frosty sway and almost fall, thrown to one side by the violence of that bucking movement. I saw the big teeth of the wolf fasten in the coat of his master, to steady himself.

And then, from the mouth of the ravine, a rifle sounded! It sounded a fraction of a second after a hornet buzz whirred past my ears. I looked down the canyon and saw that the grass fire had actually gutted the valley as quickly as all this, and that there was now a chance for the Cary clan to press in among the rocks and open fire.

I stretched out on the edge of the cliff and took aim; Taxi was beside me; only Clonmel remained ready to grab Frosty and lift him from Silver.

Taxi began to shoot. There was another shot from the mouth of the ravine. I opened on the probable spot. The thundering echoes of the guns filled the air, and the Cary rifleman who had ventured in so far ceased firing.

When I turned my head, it was because I heard a groan from Clonmel. I thought that it was because a bullet had struck him. Then I saw it was merely joyous relief as his mighty hand caught Frosty by the scruff of the neck and hauled him up to safety.

Silver followed the wolf. A knife slash severed the ropes and let the tree spring straight once more. And there we were, at last safely across the break in our trail and ready to fight for our lives on an equal footing.

What sticks in my mind most, from that moment, was the savage shouting of Chuck Cary:

"Silver—Taxi—Clonmel—Avon—we're goin' to get the whole four of you. Will Cary's goin' to eat you up like yeller coyotes! We're goin' to have your scalps!"

I only laughed, weakly and foolishly. Will Cary, compared with Silver, seemed a futile little pigmy beside a giant.

20 / A Quarrel

WE WENT UP THAT box canyon like four cats afraid of dogs. We went with Silver in the lead, and Frosty ahead of his master. I can tell you what, we were glad to have Frosty then, with ears that could hear like trumpeting noises what were soundless whispers to our human senses, and with a nose that could see through rocks and around trees or mountains. Furthermore, the wind was blowing down the canyon toward us, and, therefore, Frosty ought to have a doubly good chance of reporting the slightest danger.

But we went up that broken ravine without finding a sign of Will Cary and his manhunters!

Not that I blame them. It was one thing to look forward to lining themselves up behind shelter along the top of the cliff and quietly potting four helpless men below them. It was quite another matter to have to face in equal battle men like Silver and Taxi. At any rate, there was no sign of Will Cary.

We climbed on up the valley, got to the highest divide, and then turned down a side shoot that brought us out, once more, on the top of the circular cliffs that ran around the Cary Valley.

Jim Silver stood there for a long time, looking through the moonlight toward the Cary house, all gathered up in trees as in a gleaming cloud.

Taxi stood back with me. Clonmel was nearest to Silver.

I heard Taxi murmur: "Who is Clonmel?"

I shook my head. Then I saw that Taxi was not asking questions of me, but of himself. He was thinking aloud.

"What hold has he got on Jim?" muttered Taxi. "He can steal away Parade and Frosty, and nothing happens to him. He can act as though he had a *right* on Jim. The big, clumsy, thick-witted fool!"

That was it. Jealousy!

Well, I couldn't blame Taxi. The legend had it that he had risked his life times enough in the service of Jim Silver; the legend had it that he was the one man who had been admitted to intimate friendship by Silver. And now he had to see an interloper take his place! There was no question about it, as Clonmel stood beside Silver and dropped his great hand familiarly on the shoulder of that famous man.

"What are you thinking of, Jim?" asked Clonmel.

"You tell me, Harry," said Silver.

"You're thinking about Parade. And Christian."

Silver nodded.

"They're over there now," he said.

"They're swarming up the canyon behind us," suggested Taxi suddenly, almost angrily.

Neither Clonmel nor Silver turned to him. Clonmel simply shook his head.

"They've had enough for one night," he declared. "They've got two wounded men, and a bullet through the

111

arm of Chuck. They've missed us, and they won't want to try their luck until they have daylight to shoot by."

I saw Taxi start. I saw his hands grip hard. He was angry because of the calm surety with which Clonmel attempted to read the minds of the Cary outfit. I sympathized with him more than a little.

Silver said: "I don't think they'll press us very closely again tonight. The question is: What do they expect of us now?"

"They expect us to get back to civilization and horses as fast as we can," said Clonmel, "where we'll gather a posse and come storming up here to make trouble for 'em."

"By the time we arrived," said Silver, "they'd have everything smoothed out. Parade would be gone, and Barry Christian on him. And—perhaps Christian has gone already."

"Of course he's gone," said Taxi.

"No," answered Clonmel, "Christian is still there with them. He thinks that he has plenty of time before he makes his start for the tall timber. Nobody can follow the man who rides Parade, and Christian knows it."

There was good sense in that remark, but again I could see that Taxi was angered.

"You're right, Harry," said Silver. "Christian and Parade—they're both together somewhere inside that clump of trees. What are we going to do about it?"

There was a silence after this. The question seemed to me to have an answer that was too obvious. Of course, we would all go home and give thanks, the rest of our lives, that we had escaped from so much danger between sunset and dawn of one night.

But then the voice of Taxi said sharply, bitterly: "We'll go back there and try to get Christian. We'll go back there and try to get Parade."

I looked at him and started to laugh. The laughter broke down suddenly. Silver and Clonmel had turned toward Taxi, and Silver said:

"That's what I'll have to do, of course. But I'm going alone."

"Oh, bah!" answered Taxi. "You know that we'll have to trail along."

I stared till my eyes ached and I forgot the pain of my burned face. Go back to the Cary house? Go back to the den of snakes and lions?

"Something's upset you, Taxi," said Silver. "What's the matter?"

"Honor!" sneered Taxi. "For the honor of Jim Silver we're going back there to try to take another fall out of Barry Christian—and to get a horse! Honor be damned— it's murder, and you know it!"

A good long silence followed that remark. Finally, Clonmel said:

"Jim, you can let that pass, if you want to, but *I* won't let it pass."

"*You* won't let it pass?" snarled Taxi softly.

Great Scott, how my flesh crawled when I heard that voice of his!

"I won't let it pass," said Clonmel. "I never knew a small man in my life that ever had a big heart in him. Stay here behind, Taxi. I'll go with Jim."

"He might as well take a side of beef with him," said Taxi. "What have you ever done except steal his horse and Frosty? What have you ever done except go ahead and get yourself into trouble so that he could risk his neck getting you out?"

"Does it look like that to you?" said Clonmel. "I'll tell you something—you've said enough tonight, and it's your turn to shut up!"

Taxi cried: "I hated the sight of you when I first laid my eyes on you, and I've hated the sight of you ever since. You're a fathead and a fool. If you don't like what I say, you've got a gun—fill your hand and—"

"Taxi!" said Silver calmly.

"Are you calling me right or wrong?" demanded Taxi.

"I'm calling you wrong," said Silver.

I heard Taxi panting. I saw the panting of his quick breath. He swayed a little from side to side, and I could watch the shuddering of his body. He was for all the world like a bull terrier before it springs at a throat. And I knew that this man had killed more than once. If his

113

hand went for a gun, he would kill again, before this night was over.

And then something told me clearly, like a bursting vision of light, that if Taxi killed Clonmel, he would most certainly be slain in turn by Jim Silver. I don't know why I had such surety.

"The time's come," said Taxi, "when you pick up with every big idiot that comes across your path. You want people who'll look up to you and flatter you. You've started to be as vain as a sixteen-year-old-girl, proud of her curls. Now you choose between Clonmel and me. I'll not take another step with the pair of you!"

"If that's what he means, I'll go," said Clonmel. "I'm sorry, but he's worth a lot more to you than I am."

"Wait a moment," said Silver.

We all waited. It was a horrible suspense. Silver was staring straight at Taxi, not speaking a word, and Taxi, his body still wavering and uncertainly poised by the greatness of his emotion, stared back at Silver.

"I'll go," said Clonmel suddenly. "So long, Jim!"

He held out his hand. Instead of taking it, Silver laid his touch lightly on the arm of the giant.

"Stay here with me," he said, looking always not at Clonmel but at Taxi.

Well, that was it then—he had made his choice!

I admit that I was staggered. Silver was the man who could do no wrong—and yet he was casting aside for the sake of a stranger the devotion that Taxi had given to him so many times!

"Well," said Taxi, in a voice that was not much more than a whisper, "that's about enough. I'll be getting along. So long, boys. Good luck to you!"

He turned his back and walked slowly away up the gulch.

"Tell him, Jim!" cried Clonmel. "Tell him—"

"Be quiet," said Silver, with iron in his voice. "I won't speak a word to persuade him."

"But don't let him go thinking that—" began Clonmel.

"It's better this way," answered Silver.

He stood there calm and still, and I saw Taxi disappear around the first elbow turn.

All of this had been quiet enough, but somehow it seemed to me a lot more terrible than all that had happened since we first entered the Cary Valley and Chuck Cary had made a prisoner of me.

There was something wrong about it all, and my heart ached right up in my throat.

"Ah, Jim," muttered Clonmel, "why did you do it? Why did you do it to Taxi of all the men in the world?"

"Because," said Silver, "he should not have suspected me. If there's suspicion in a friend, there's lead in gold. There are other reasons, too."

"Tell me what they are then!" I exclaimed. "People have a right to know the truth about you, Silver!"

"I'll tell you what they are," said Silver. "That man has followed me through hell-fire. He'll still follow me if I give him the right word. But I won't give him the word. There may be safety for one man, on the trail that I have to follow, but there can't be safety for two. Not in the end. And it's better for Taxi to leave me now."

"Ah, Jim, but it's hard," said Clonmel. "It's breaking my heart to think of Taxi going off like that!"

"Your heart, Harry?" said Silver, in a curiously calm voice. "Is it breaking *your* heart?"

"I mean," explained Clonmel, "that if—"

"Let's not talk," answered Silver, more gently than ever. "I'd rather not talk for a while."

I was glad of the silence. As it lasted, it gave me a chance to expand all the ideas that I had of Jim Silver. It gave me a chance to look at him and realize what he was. And all the long moment that followed he kept growing in my conception until I could see him for what he was—a man without cruelty or unkindness or selfishness or smallness in his heart.

No wonder that Taxi at last had broken away, I thought. To associate even for a short time with Jim Silver was to realize before long all of one's faults, set off by all the greatness of his soul.

It still seems a strange thing to me, when I consider that scene—and the strangest part of it all, at the time, was the quiet of Silver. I did not know him so well then.

I thought that Silver, like all men, would have to make a noise when he was greatly moved. But I was wrong.

After a time, he turned about and looked across the plain toward the house of Cary.

"I'm going over there," he said. "I think one man could do what three could not. But if there's something inside you that makes you want to come along, I can't honorably send you back. You'd better say so long, though."

He waved his hand to both of us, and then started along the edge of the cliff, toward a gap in the distance that promised an easy way of getting down to the level of the plain below.

Big Clonmel, without more than a moment's hesitation, strode out after Frosty and the master, but I waited until all three were out of sight among the rocks.

Then it seemed to me that the dying noise of the footfalls was striking right in upon my heart. I pulled myself together with a jump, and ran suddenly after them.

21 / The Revelation

WE WENT DOWN off the highland to the plain. We went down like pigeons among hawks, like small boats into a sea of pirates. We went down on foot into that land where savages worse than Indians might be cruising about on their swift horses. And if a rasher act were ever undertaken, at least I've never heard of the attempt.

You may say that all of us had our eyes open, though as a matter of fact I think it is only fair to state that no mind was working calmly and clearly except that of Jim Silver.

He knew the odds and he had suggested the expedition. The rest of us followed him simply because pride and shame are stronger than fear, in most of us. But I know that I went with the feeling that a knife was pressed against my throat every step of the way.

There was no such thing as skirting about the plain and trying to get at the house from a favorable angle. Silver seemed to trust everything to chance, in this stage of the business. He simply headed straight forward toward the trees, and the only precaution he took was that Frosty was sent out perhaps a hundred yards in the lead.

We were half-way over the plain when Frosty came racing back toward us. He stopped and whined in front of Silver, and Silver looked carefully down at him, as though he were listening to words. My hair fairly lifted when Silver straightened and actually laughed.

"Rabbits!" he said. "Frosty has spotted a warren—that's all!"

It was as though he had understood the whined language of the beast, but, of course, it was no such matter. I dare say that since there are not so many species of game, the action of Frosty in reporting them, his degree of excitement, and his whole behavior would tell his master just about what his nose had read on the ground.

At any rate, we went straight on, with Frosty again leading us, and we came without a halt closer and closer to the trees, until we could see the glints of lamplight that reached out from the house. So we entered the region of shadow and halted there for a moment.

I was wishing for Taxi more than for anything else. Taxi could open a lock as any other man could crack a walnut. Taxi knew how to make his feet travel over dead leaves with scarcely a rustle. For night work how could there be another man in the world to compare with him?

That was what I was thinking when I stood with the other two inside the rim of trees.

Silver said in a lowered voice: "They're inside, having a good time. But a few of them are behind the house. You hear their voices sounding in the open air? Well, those are probably the ones who are guarding Parade. Christian knows enough not to take any chances, and that means that perhaps they're keeping a strick watch on their whole house as well as on the corral where Parade may be."

As he read off the sounds and diagnosed the character

117

of them, I listened more intently. It was true that there were voices sounding muffled, from inside the house, and others that came to us more largely and freely from the open air behind the house. When we went on, we found it was exactly as Silver had suggested. We rounded the horse, still keeping safely back in the trees, and behind it we saw a corral with four lanterns put up on corner posts, hanging just inside them so that the flames were throwing shadows toward the outside and light toward the inside. And inside the corral they picked out and flared over the body of the chestnut stallion.

I saw that horse as I never saw a horse before or afterward. Because the question I asked myself at the time was: Should three sane men risk their lives in order to redeem a stolen animal? But as I stared at the glorious beauty and strength of the stallion, I decided that we were not foolish and that it was almost better that the three of us should die than that Barry Christian should continue to own the horse.

But how were we to get to it?

Silver drew us back into the trees. Then, when it was safe for him to speak, he said:

"You see how it is. Even if we were thirty instead of three, it would be almost ridiculous for us to try to get at Parade. They've arranged it very cleverly. The light of the lanterns only hits the horse. The guards are posted away from the corral in the shadow. If we try to rush Parade, we'll get nothing but bullets. I could whistle to him and bring him out here in three jumps, but they've hobbled his feet!"

That was true. As Silver himself confessed the impossibility of doing anything by a direct raid on the horse, I felt a greater and greater relief. It was almost like getting permission to go home. As he made his pause, I even said:

"Well, then we'd better get out of here!"

"I think you had," said Silver. "What comes next is a thing that silence will help along more than numbers. You'd better go back, Avon. Good-by. Good-by, Harry."

"What's up now?" asked Harry.

"I'm not sure. But it's nothing that you could help in," said Jim Silver. "Good-by to both of you. I'll be seeing you later."

As he talked, I saw a shadowy something move behind a tree. I snatched up my rifle to the level and aimed at the spot where I had seen the ghost stir.

"There's something—there!" I gasped.

Even with the moonlight from above and the thin rays of lamplight from the side, there was still only the faintest hint at illumination. The three of us stood rigid, while Silver, with a sweep of his hand, sent Frosty forward.

I saw the great beast drop on his belly and crawl toward the tree. I was certain that something was concealed behind the trunk. There had been no opportunity for it to escape, whatever it was. I waited, bracing myself, to hear the savage snarl and see the leap of the wolf. Instead, as Frosty slid around the tree, I saw him straighten to his feet and then heard him whine, a guttural sound that was as close to kindness as he knew how to make.

Immediately after that, the voice of Taxi said, with what seemed to me unnecessary loudness: "I couldn't keep away from the party, Jim."

He stepped out before us. I never was so glad to hear a voice, never so glad to see a form, in all my days.

"Ah, Taxi—" said Silver, starting forward.

"Stay where you are!" commanded Taxi sharply. "I'll come all the way."

Silver halted. Taxi walked up to him and held out his hand.

"I was wrong, Jim," he said. "It was Clonmel. And I was wrong. If you think more of him than you do of me, it's because he's the better man. I want you to take me back."

Jim Silver gripped the hand quickly. Then he said:

"Clonmel is not a better man. There's no better man in the world than Taxi. But he's my brother."

"Brother?" gasped Taxi.

"Brother?" I breathed.

"I would have told you both before," said Silver, "but I've been having an idea that if people know he's my brother, they'll be apt to follow him with some of the hate that they owe me."

"I guessed it!" groaned Taxi. "At the start I guessed it. Not that he was your brother. But I saw the flash of the likeness. Something jumped like a spark inside me! Ah, what a fool I am. Clonmel, I beg your pardon for the talk I handed out to you."

Clonmel chuckled a little.

"You could say worse than that, and I'd take it with a smile," he said. "I'm that glad to have you back with us, Taxi. Tell Jim that whatever idea he has in mind, he's wrong, and ought to forget it!"

Just then, a braying sound of laughter came out of the house with such a raucous blast that it sounded as though mocking voices were moving toward us through the trees.

Taxi merely said: "What Jim decides is what I decide."

Silver went on: "I can't hold back. I've got to go ahead. I'm going into the house and try to kill Christian. He's in there with the men who are laughing."

"All right," said Taxi, after a moment. "I go with you. You may need me to open the doors."

"And I go," said Clonmel.

"You stay away," said Silver. "An open-air raid to get Parade, that's one thing. To tackle that house with all the poison inside it, that's a different matter altogether!"

"I go!" said Clonmel.

"Harry," said Silver, "you have a father and a mother."

"The same ones that you have," answered Clonmel.

"I've been the same as dead to them these many years," said Silver.

"There's never a day that they're not praying for you! Why else was I sent out to try to find you?" said Clonmel.

"God forgive me if I bring you to the end of your trail!" groaned Silver. "But I think that this may be the last night for either Christian or me! I'm going straight on to the house and take the luck that's planned for me. Any one of you can follow me that wishes."

He turned about sharply. A wave of his hand brought Frosty to his heels. And so Silver walked ahead of us through the trees. I saw Taxi and Clonmel walk on behind him, side by side. For my part, I wanted to remain behind, but a devil of the perverse inside me drew my heavy feet after them once more.

22 / Den of Danger

SUPPOSE YOU WERE TO walk up to a lion which is wide awake, but whose glances, so far, have failed to notice you? That was the way I felt when I walked up with the other three, and Frosty, toward the Cary house. It was like a face, the face of a monstrous and dangerous beast. And though some windows and doors were blank, others were rimmed about or lighted over from the inside. And the whole place swelled and stirred and hummed with life, and every atom of that life was poisonous to us.

We went up to a door at the side of the first wing, where not a light was showing, and Taxi bent over the heavy steel lock for only a moment. Then that door opened soundlessly. He pulled out a little pocket torch and flashed the ray of light like knife strokes across and across the darkness inside. Two or three glimpses and he seemed to know where everything was. But as for me, it was a question of following a leader, when we got inside that room. Clonmel came last and shut the door behind us.

At once I was breathing the hot, still air of the house, defiled with odors of cookery. There was the exact sense of having been shut into the lions' den—not sleeping lions, mind you, but beasts which simply had failed to notice us, so far. There was only one comfort, which was that the floor was the naked earth, and there were no creaking boards to trouble us.

A footfall ran like thunder through the second story, clumped down some stairs, and thudded quietly over the ground.

By the sound the runner made, I could conjure up the picture of the man—tall, wide-shouldered, powerful dark-eyed—a true Cary. Every man of them all was fit to tie me into knots, I felt sure.

We went through two or three more dark rooms with only an occasional flash from the torch of Taxi to show us the way, then leaving us to struggle through the murk, trusting our hands more than our memories to guide us past the clumsy, home-made furniture.

We were making on toward a center of much noise. The last flash of the electric torch had showed me Frosty slinking at the heels of his master—and then a door before us was jerked open, and a great tide of light poured over us.

I was blinded, stunned by the brightness. Then a grip on my arm called me back to myself and drew me slowly aside. And now I could see that a tall young Cary was standing there in the doorway with his head turned, looking back toward his companions who were scattered about a long table, drinking and smoking. The big earthenware jugs held moonshine whisky, I could guess; and the water-colored liquid that stood in the glasses was faintly stained with yellow. Three or four lanterns were scattered irregularly down the table which was composed of big ax-hewn planks laid over heavy trestles. The feet of the trestles had sunk, with weight and time, into the ground. So the table was rather low and made it easy for the Carys to spread their elbows at the board, or for some of them to lean back in their chairs and rest their spurred heels on the wood.

They looked to me like a gang of pirates before, not after, sacking a town. Money or blood—they had an equal thirst for both.

Women were going about in the room. There was one for almost every man, and each was tending the wants of a male, pouring his whisky, or fetching him what he wished to eat. Some of the men tore at joints of meat; others were eating bread and cheese. And I noticed that none of the women sat down in the presence of their masters.

The fellow at the door was calling out something—I

forget what—to one of his friends, and there was a general roar of laughter that beat and thundered against my ears. Then the man turned and walked right through the darkness of the room in which we were ranged back against the walls. He was carrying an unlighted lantern. He was still chuckling to himself over his last remark. And though we could see him so clearly, he could not make us out. Once he turned his head and looked straight at me, but I suppose that the glare from which he had just come dimmed his eyes a good deal. At any rate, he stumbled against a chair before he got out of the room, so he paused, and lighted his lantern then and there.

As I saw the spurt of the match flame, and heard the lantern chimney pushed screeching up on its guards of rusted wire, I made sure that we would be discovered the next instant. I saw then that Taxi's automatic was out and covering the fellow. He had only to turn in order to see us now—and die before us!

But instead of turning, he rubbed his shin where he had collided with the chair, swore a little, and then opened the next door and went on, the lantern swinging at his side and his great shadow sweeping back and forth across the opposite wall.

He was gone from view and hearing in another moment, but now we were left in an open throat of danger, so to speak.

That passer-by had left wide the door into the dining room. He had gone on, I couldn't tell where, and he might return at any moment. And in the meantime, fifteen or more armed men were sitting there in the lantern light, ready to answer any alarm. Furthermore, they were all descendants of the old man, and they all looked worthy of the name.

I picked out young Chuck at once. He was sitting at the head of the table, facing the door, and this was evidently a place of honor that was accorded him for what he had done—or tried to do—that day. In fact, if Taxi's snap shot had not made him drop his rifle after he fired his first bullet, it was plain enough that young Chuck would have easily held all our lives in the hollow of his hand.

He had one arm tied up in a blood-stained sling, and he was drinking his moonshine and smoking a pipe like any of the grown men. Apparently he was considered to have gained his place among the ranks of the mature warriors.

But what were we to do?

I kept waiting for Silver to give a signal of some sort, either to charge forward through the doorway—a crazy proceeding—or to withdraw as stealthily as possible through the other open door. However, Silver crouched quietly in a corner, with the dim glimmer of the gray wolf beside him. I was on the opposite side of the room with Taxi, and I could see the green, glowing eyes of Frosty.

There was a pounding of hoofs outside, and then, through another entrance out of my ken, Will Cary and four other men walked into the room.

Some of the others jumped up. A volley of questions rained around the head of Will Cary.

He stood up there at the head of the table, near Chuck, and faced that crowd frankly and fearlessly.

"I didn't get hands on them, if that's what you want to know," he said. "I'll tell you the reason why I didn't lay hands on them. I was too scared. So were the boys with me. We were five, and they were four. Two of that four were Silver and Taxi. We didn't have the nerve to face 'em."

He made a pause and looked boldly around the table.

"Do I hear anybody sound off with the idea that they would have done differently?"

Heads turned a bit this way and that, but the side glances did not last long. The Carys looked back at Will, and after a moment there was a sort of general grunting. Whatever they were thinking, no one cared to stand and blame Will for what he and his companions had done in the way of flinching from duty.

Will Cary said, when he saw that he had made his point: "I'm sorry about it. I've got reasons for wanting them all wiped out. Better reasons than the rest of you, maybe. But the fact is, they're too good for us unless we've got numbers on 'em. Jim Silver didn't get a reputation for nothing. Neither did Taxi. When I saw that we weren't going to get any advantage of them, with that wolf sneaking on ahead of 'em to spy us out, I decided to quit. And even if I had decided to go ahead, the boys with me wouldn't have budged. They's seen how Silver could shoot by starlight. They didn't hanker to see how he could shoot by moonlight."

He broke off to ask: "How's Bud and Cleve?"

His father, Dean Cary, spoke up before the others, saying: "Bud's laid out with a slug through his right hip. Cleve's down with a bullet through both legs."

"There you've got it," said Will Cary. "You fellows may think that it's chance, but my idea is that Silver *aimed* low. He doesn't take life till he has to. That's what people say about him. And it's true. If he'd wanted to take life, Bud and Cleve would have some lead inside them, by this time, and I guess you all know that I'm right!"

Any way you take it, that speech of Will Cary's was pretty free and easy, and he finished it off by lifting a big jug of moonshine, pouring out a shot, and tossing off the drink. He coughed and choked over it a little, afterward.

"It takes a strong man to be a Cary!" he said, and laughed a little.

I rather liked Will Cary, just then. I mean I liked his frankness, and the suggestion that he saw some of the faults of the clan as clearly as I could, even.

But trouble came down on Will's head, a minute later, when a door squeaked open and I heard the voice of the old man.

He said huskily, with a sort of ironic cheer: "Well, boys, here you all are, all kind of spread out havin' your good time. Havin' your nip of whisky and your eats. Well, well, them that work hard has gotta eat hard, too. And look at the work you've all been and done today! Look at what you've put behind you! Look at all the brave things you've done! You've caught old Bill Avon and Clonmel and locked 'em up—and lost 'em! You've had your hands on Frosty and Parade—and you've lost Frosty. You've had Jim Silver and Taxi and the other two lying in the palms of your hands—and you've lost 'em all. And

125

after all of that work, it ain't no wonder that you gotta kind of relax for a minute and take things easy and remember that all work and no play makes Jack a dull boy. I don't wonder that you're sittin' here and makin' your fingers all thumbs with booze, in spite of the fact that Silver and Taxi are right here in the house this minute!"

When he said that, a shooting chill went up out of my eyes and froze my forehead. Every one of those Carys came to his feet with a shout, and the squeals of the women tingled over the noise.

The old man came swaying into my view, leaning his arm over the shoulder of Maria and peering around at the men.

With the bright wet stem of his pipe, he kept pointing to this man and that.

"I mean, there ain't no reason why Silver shouldn't be here!" he said. "There ain't no good guard put out. There ain't any preparations made to catch him."

A gray-headed, greasy-faced Cary of the second generation said; "Pa, not even Jim Silver is comin' back here. Even Silver has had enough of the Carys to last him for a while. If he *does* come back, he'll come for Parade, and we got that hoss plastered all around with guards. What more d'you ask?"

"That's right, Danny," said the terrible old man. "You tell us what Jim Silver is thinkin' about. You figger and plan on what's in his head, because you oughta know. It's brains like yours that knowed he couldn't get into the smoke-house. You didn't see that the tree behind the smoke-house give him his chance of climbin' up on top of the roof, but outside of that, you figgered everything out fine to keep them two in the smoke-house. All you done was to let 'em get away.

"And right this minute, if he's got the brains of a gnat, Silver oughta be back here in this house listenin' to what I say and laughin' up his sleeve at you. Because he oughta be able to see that the Carys ain't what they used to be. They used to be men, but they've fell off from that a whole lot. And Silver ain't quite blind. He's able to see a few things, I take it. He's got the name of havin'

126

eyes. Maybe he's right here in the house now, in that west room in the top story, layin' a knife into Barry Christian that's done us the honor of comin' here and chummin' with us and trustin' his life in our hands. M'ria, close that there door. They's a draft blowin' in on me."

Maria slipped from under his arm and came to our open door. She stood there for an instant, staring—and her eyes were fixed on the huge figure of Clonmel, who stood pressed into a corner. By the wideness of her eyes, by the ripple that ran through her body, I knew that she saw him clearly. I waited for the yell of terror and the rush of the armed men.

Instead of that, she stepped back and quietly closed the door so that the darkness was suddenly thick through the room.

I heard the whisper of Taxi saying: "Get ready to meet 'em with lead."

Taxi had noticed what I had noticed, then!

But the whisper of Jim Silver added instantly: "She saw Harry—and she won't tell!"

I could not believe it, but the long moment was drawn out and out and still there was no outbreak in the next room. I heard the voice of the old man begin to drawl on, once more. Then I knew it was true, and that the girl was holding her hand!

When we had worked our way out of that room, I felt as though we had seen the fire and had been in the flames, and that we would certainly get out of the house as fast as possible. But, of course, that was not in the mind of Silver. Taxi, with a couple of glints of light, gave us our location in the next room, and I heard Silver say to him:

"Christian's in the west room, on the second floor— that's this way, Taxi. Go first. You've got the quietest feet."

That was true. Taxi could move like a shadow. He went before us, lighting what lay ahead of us with the thin, quick winkings of his torch. And we followed. Silver was, of course, next in line, with Frosty beside him; Clonmel followed, and I was the last in place as in importance. I was badly frightened, but I remember wondering at the noiselessness of the wolf. The big claws on his feet never scratched or rattled on the steps.

We got up into the hallway above, and it was as crooked a passage as I ever saw. I suppose that was because the additions to the first cabin had been made so irregularly. The hall twisted this way and that and dodged up and down repeatedly as it rose or fell to new levels.

We were well down that hall towards the west end of the crazy building when a door opened right at the foot of the hall and the figure of a tall man stepped out.

It was Christian. I knew him by an indescribable something connected with his carriage of head and shoulders, something proud and confident that distinguished him from all other men I've ever seen.

He came straight down into the blackness of the hallway, after he had shut his door. And I braced myself for the shock when he reached us and Silver should strike him down. Or would Jim Silver take even Christian by surprise and in the darkness, like this?

The footfalls of Christian stopped. He knocked at a door, apparently, and a woman's voice sang out for him to enter.

He pulled the door open, and the light from within streamed out against him.

"Hello, Julie," said Christian. "Hello, Sue."

Not the voice of Julie Perigord answered, but another woman saying harshly:

"I thought you'd be turning up to have a look at the beauty. She's got the looks and the eyes to snag even Barry Christian, eh?"

"Run along, Sue," said Christian. "I want to talk with her."

"So I run along, do I?" said Sue. "And how am I to know that you won't be running the opposite way, pretty quick, and the gal along with you? I've seen you giving the eye to her. I ain't blind, Christian."

"Do you think, Sue," said Christian, "that we would run away from the Carys? Do you think that we'd be such fools?"

"I'll trust a man as far as I can keep a forty-foot rope tied to him," said Sue. "When there's a gal with a face like Julie's mixed up in it, I won't even trust him that far. Understand what I'm saying?"

"I understand," said Christian. "And you don't remember, do you, that Julie Perigord is engaged to Will Cary? What the matter with you, Sue? You're a bit rattled, aren't you?"

"Her and Will Cary—that was calf love—or no love at all," said Sue. "Well, I'm going to get out and leave you two alone, but I'll bet I catch the devil for it, in the wind-up."

23 / Christian's Idea

I HEARD A CHAIR pushed back in that room, and the flashlight of Taxi at the same instant glinted on the knob of a door just beside him. He pushed that door open, and we faded into the dark of a room, all of us, while the firm footfall of Sue came out of the next door and turned down the hall.

She kept on talking as she moved.

"Treat him good, Julie," she called. "It ain't every gal in this world that gets a smile from Barry Christian. Mostly he don't smile except on gents with loaded wallets."

She laughed. The sound of her laughter passed away down the hall, and went suddenly dim around a corner. The creaking of her footfall still sounded clearly, moving out of hearing only step by step.

There was only a thin partition between our room and the next. When Christian spoke, it was startlingly as though he were in the darkness on our side of the wall.

"Here we are at last, Julie," he said.

A thickness of silence followed that remark.

"Just thinking things over, or damning me a little, Julie?" he asked.

"Not a little," said the voice of the girl, speaking for the first time.

A breath was caught somewhere close to me. That would be Clonmel, I could imagine.

"And yet," said Christian, "the fact is that you ought to be leaning on me, Julie. There's no good chance for you here. Do you know just how bad your chance really is?"

"I'd like to know," said Julie Perigord.

I liked the way she talked, quietly, with a world of that composure which is like a reserve of strength.

"You'll have to marry a Cary," said Christian. "Does that sound good to you?"

"I won't have to marry a Cary," said the girl. "They know that I've come up here for a different reason."

"Because of that big fellow? Because of Clonmel? Yes, they realize that, and that's the reason they have to make sure of you. You've seen a great deal too much, and you know a great deal too much. You've got to be a Cary— or else you're not going to be anything at all!"

"You think that they'd knock me over the head?" asked Julie.

"No, I don't think that. The old man doesn't like killings. Just a few, now and then, to show that his young men are the right stuff. And he wants most of those killings to take place a good distance from home. But there are ways of persuading a girl to change her mind."

"Are there?" asked Julie.

"For instance—" began Christian.

"I don't want to know what they are," she declared.

"Let it drop, then. I simply want to make sure that you understand."

"I understand they're savages," said Julie.

"Then that leads me straight on to a logical conclusion," said Christian. "I'm rather tired of a lonely life. There's only one way you can dodge out of this place— and that's with my help. What do you think of the idea?"

"Elope with Barry Christian?" said Julie.

"That's the idea. You may have some bad ideas about me, Julie. I deserve a good many of the bad ideas, at that. But there are some decent streaks in me, too. What do you say?"

"On the whole," said Julie, "I suppose I ought to thank you."

"I don't ask for thanks."

"I'm afraid you won't get them, either," said the girl.

"You're going to be hard on me, are you?" asked Christian. It was a wonderful thing to hear the plaintiveness creep into his voice. And what a voice it was! Listening to him on the far side of the wall, I could not help forgetting what I knew about him. Even the nearness of Silver to me in the dark was not entirely enough to keep the truth about Barry Christian in my mind.

"I won't be hard on you," said Julie. "It simply can't be that way. You see?"

"You'd rather stay with the Cary tribe? Is that the truth?"

"That's the truth."

"What makes you detest me so, Julie?"

"Why, I've heard a good deal about you. At second-hand, so to speak."

"How do you mean that?" asked Christian.

"I mean, I've heard what Jim Silver has been through on your trail."

"He's a head-hunter," said Christian. "Are you going to believe all the fairy tales that they tell about Silver?"

"If I couldn't believe in Jim Silver," said Julie, "I don't think that I'd want to believe in *anything*."

"Ah, there's your handsome giant—there's Clonmel," said Christian. "What about him?"

"I love him," said Julie, so quietly that the force of what she said only struck me afterwards. "And love isn't exactly the same as belief. I don't know Harry Clonmel. But I know Jim Silver. Every decent person in the mountains knows Jim Silver and has to believe in him."

"Are you going to throw me out like this?" said Christian. "Isn't it being a little foolish?"

There was a sound like a whispering. My friends were rising from the floor where we had been crouching. The ray from Taxi's torch showed us the door. Taxi opened it. We passed out into the hall, arranged ourselves in a half moon, and then Taxi opened the next door, softly but suddenly.

131

It made a soft, rushing noise of wind as the draft sucked out after the door. That whispering noise made Christian turn his head and see Jim Silver on the threshold.

24 / End of the Trail

RIGHT BEHIND SILVER, looming above him, was the half-naked giant, Clonmel. And on the other side of Silver stood the slender form of Taxi. As for me, I didn't count, and I was about out of sight, anyway. But those three must have looked to Christian like three devils out of hell.

The sight lifted him to his feet, slowly, as though an invisible hand had grabbed him by the hair of the head and raised him. I think there was hardly a man in the world with a colder nerve than Barry Christian, but now he turned white. His face was always pale; now it became like clear stone, and his eyes were dark streaks.

Against these odds, he was perfectly helpless.

Julie Perigord got up from the table, also. She looked at the trio in the doorway, and I saw her smile. There were not three men there. For her, there was only Clonmel.

Silver said: "You can put your hands up, Barry."

"Thanks, Jim," said Christian. "I must tell you that if you take another step, I'll yell. You'll have me dead, but the Cary tribe will be picking your bones before my body is cold."

That was true enough. I could see that with a fellow as cool as Christian there was only one thing to do.

And then I heard Silver saying: "Do you think that I'll back out of the house without you, Barry?"

"Why not?" answered Christian. "You'll have the girl. To a fellow of your character, Silver, the righting of a wrong ought to be enough. Tut, tut! You won't leave the poor child here in the hands of the brutal Carys, will you? Not if I know the noble character of Jim Silver."

You see, he was entire master of himself again, after the first deadliness of the shock. There he stood and sneered at his great enemy. I could understand then why Christian had been able to stand out so long against Silver. It was because the man was as great a power for evil as Silver was for good.

"Besides," said Christian, "you have to think about your friends. A young hero, there—Clonmel—and my old companion, Taxi—the lad you saved from the underworld and brought right up into the honest sunshine of life—to say nothing of that flat-faced mug of a Bill Avon, that I see in the rear of the trouble—you don't want to throw them all away, Jim. And most assuredly they'll die with you, if you take another step. I shout, Jim—and the final battle begins!"

It was convincing. Not so convincing as I write it down, but utterly convincing if you had been there to see the flash of his eye and the sneer of his lip.

But Silver took the step forward!

"Better wait there, hadn't you?" said Christian.

The calmness of the pair was what drove knives of ice through me.

"You're a very intelligent fellow, Barry," said Silver, "and you might win out with most people. There's only one valuable thing that I know about you—that is that you value your hide. But if the girl has to become a Cary; if Taxi and Clonmel and poor Bill Avon have to die with me—it's worth the price to wipe you off the earth!"

And he went straight up to Christian.

I saw the lips of Christian part. I saw his chest heave as he drew in a breath. I squinted my eyes against the shock of hearing the cry that would be the death signal for all of us. But the cry did not come. Silver simply took hold of Christian by the wrist and held in his other hand a Colt revolver, by the barrel, so that it would make an efficient club.

"All right, Jim," said Christian. "It looks as though you win this trick, for the moment. How you'd like to smash the gun into my face, eh?"

He chuckled softly. It seemed to me that I could live a thousand years and never come across a stranger thing than that laugh of Christian's, as he confronted Silver.

"Fan him, Taxi," said Silver.

The slim, deft hands of Taxi dipped into the clothes of Christian.

They brought out two man-sized Colts and a little double-barreled pistol hardly larger than a man's hand, but able to throw a fatal bullet across the width of a room, no doubt. It was hitched up the arm of Christian with a strong elastic. There was a long knife that was worn just inside the front of his belt. It had a flat, heavily weighted handle, so that it could be used either for throwing or hand-to-hand fighting. As I looked at the four weapons, I had a grisly, a sickening sense that all of them had taken lives.

There was a wallet, also, that Taxi produced. It was fat. He opened it up, and I saw two thick sheaves of bills, each sheaf filling a side of the wallet. The man was carrying a good-sized fortune around with him.

Silver said hastily: "Put the wallet back, Taxi." There was a quick disgust in his voice.

Christian interpreted calmly: "Blood money, Taxi. None of that shall ever touch the pure fingers of Jim Silver. Blood money, my boy!"

He chuckled again. I had a feeling that the cool devil was almost enjoying this excitement.

Silver tied Christian. He did it in a strange way. He simply wound a twine cord around his wrists and then put a loop of the twine around his neck. That left Christian free to move, but it meant that he could not move fast. His hands were about helpless, and no man could run or jump freely, tied in that way.

Then we four left the house, taking Christian with us, and Julie.

Nothing happened, of all the things that *could* have happened. We simply went down to the head of the first stairs, and down those stairs through a door that stood open for us, and so out under the stars. I had a crazy desire to screech and laugh.

We walked straight away from the house and got safely

into the first patch of brush. As it closed around us, rays of dim light came from the cabin and struck all about us, throwing wild patterns of shadow over us.

And I heard the voice of the old man, saying: "Keep on watch all night. Mind you, keep stirring. And every time a star blinks, think that it may be Jim Silver about to drop out of the sky!"

Yes, the old man had finished stirring up his boys, and now he was posting them on guard. He was just a little too late. If he had been ten years younger, he would have had them out on post well before we got away from the place, I dare say. And I had a shivering suspicion that, when he was a youngster, he might have been a full match for Jim Silver and all the rest of us.

I looked back through the leaves and I saw the old man's tall, straight, but fragile figure, supported as usual against the slender strength of Maria. The Cary outfit was scattered here and there, taking up positions about the house.

Then I heard the old man say: "What the devil's the matter with you, M'ria? What are you bawlin' about?"

Maria's sobbing voice answered: "Shut your mouth! Don't speak to me. Don't you *never* speak to me!"

I wondered what would happen after that speech, but to my amazement, the old man simply broke out into his husky laughter.

"That's the way I like to hear a gal talk," he said. "That's the good old Cary blood speakin' up loud and bold. M'ria, I'm sorry that you ain't a man. You would 'a' been worth all the rest of the gang, I can tell you!"

The girl said nothing. I heard her catch her breath on another sob. That was all.

I wondered, then, whether she cried because she thought Clonmel was still in the house, being hemmed in, or whether she guessed that he was already gone. I still wonder about it, but I imagine that the second guess was right.

Then I had to turn and walk on after my companions.

We went through the trees for a good distance, and down a hollow, and across a rivulet of water, and over a hill into another wood until we reached a small clearing among the trees. Every step of that journey I was thank-ing my stars that we were putting distance between us and the house of the Carys.

But here we stopped, and Silver said to Taxi:

"Will the sound of guns carry from here to the house?"

"Not the noise of revolvers," said Taxi. "Not with the wind hanging where it is."

Silver looked carefully about him. When he had fin-ished his survey, he finally said:

"Well, it seems all right to me. Taxi, turn Christian's hands loose, and give him one of his Colts."

"Why?" asked Taxi.

"Because," said Silver, "the time has come for us to fight the old fight out to a finish. Either Christian or I come to the end of the trail, here."

25 / A Night Trip

WHEN I HEARD SILVER say this, I looked steadily at Chris-tian, but the moonlight struck such a shadow across his face that I could not see his features clearly or judge his expression. I only remember that by the dignity of his carriage and that peculiarly proud outline of the high head, he seemed perfectly at ease.

Silver told us to pile all our weapons under a tree and stand a little distance from them. We did as he told us. I felt a trembling awe when I thought that I had come to see the end of the long feud.

I remember how Frosty sat down and pointed his nose up in the air as though he were about to bay the moon, and how the black shadows of the western trees lay out on the sun-bleached whiteness of the grass. Then Silver said:

"You can pick the sort of weapons, Barry. Rifles or revolvers—or bare hands. Whatever you say."

When he came to "bare hands," something came into

his voice that I can't describe. It was simply one rush of savagery to the throat, and the sound of the voice gave me the creeps. It made me realize how utterly he hated and loathed Barry Christian.

Then I heard Christian say, as calmly as ever: "I won't fight you, Silver."

I heard it, but I couldn't believe it.

Neither could Silver, it seemed. He walked up and gave Christian one of the revolvers which had been taken from him. Christian took it in a limp hand.

"It's no good, Jim," he said. "I won't fight you."

"You don't understand," explained Silver. "You see not one of my friends has a weapon of any kind. All the stuff is piled under that tree. If you drop me, you can get out before they even reach the guns."

"Frosty would pull me down if I ran," said Christian.

"A bullet would stop Frosty," answered Silver. "Or I'll tie him."

Christian simply shook his head. He turned a little. The moon struck aslant across his face, and I could study the expression easily. There was no contortion, as of a man passing through a great emotion. He was perfectly calm, I'll swear.

"It's no good, Jim," he said. There was something like affection in his voice, as when one explains a thing to a small child. "I won't fight you."

"Knife, or hand, or gun—you can make your choice," said Silver.

He was the one who was passing a little out of control. His voice quivered.

"You're a shade stronger, a shade faster, a shade keener than I am," said Christian. "You can murder me, Jim, but I won't fight you on equal terms."

"You want a—" Silver choked on what he was about to say. He walked up to Christian and struck him across the face with the back of his hand and then leaped away. I saw Christian crouch a bit. I made sure that he would jerk up his gun that instand and fire. Silver, tense as a cat, was ready for the first move. But gradually Christian straightened.

"No," he said slowly. "Not even that!"

I heard Silver groan, as he said: "You wait for a chance to put a bullet through my back. Is that it?"

"The way one wild beast treats another. That's exactly it," said Christian.

It was the strangest scene I ever imagined. My mind still turns back to it with a shock—a sort of horror. For here were two fearless men. You couldn't say that fear was what was working in Christian. It was simply that he was logical. He was convinced that Silver was his master in a fight and he would not throw his life away.

"It has to be murder, then?" said Silver.

"Not murder, Jim," said Harry Clonmel. "It's an execution. I'll shoot him down, if you won't. It's only doing justice on the dog."

He turned to go to the tree where the guns were piled.

"Wait a moment," said Silver. "Barry," he pleaded, "will you stand up like a man and fight?"

"Not a stroke," said Christian. "Pick me any other man in the world, and I'll give him odds and beat him. But even now that you're excited, you're a little too fast for me. Just the hair's-breadth that means a killing. You can murder me, but I won't fight."

You see, it was beyond a mere question of shame. And he used that word "murder" repeatedly—to Silver the most horrible word in the language.

"You lie," said Taxi. "You won't give odds, and you won't have to give odds. I'll take you on."

"Will you?" said Christian.

"I'll take you on," answered Taxi.

"Take him then," said Silver.

"Give him your gun," said Christian eagerly. "It's a bargain, Jim. If I beat him—if I down him, I'm free? I'll get Parade back for you, if that's what you want. After that—I'm free?"

Silver was breathing so hard that I could hear the sound half a dozen paces away, where I stood.

"Are you willing, Taxi?" he asked.

"Yes," said Taxi, "but I'll take my own automatic."

"Get it!" said Silver.

Taxi went over and got his own gun. He began to whistle a little, half under his breath, like a man whose mind is preoccupied. He came back and stood in front of Christian, about eight or nine steps from him. I began to feel sick at the stomach. Frosty ran to his master and lay across Silver's feet, exactly as though he realized that Silver was not going to fight.

"Ready!" said Christian.

"I'm ready any time," said Taxi.

Clonmel broke in: "After you, it ought to be my chance at him, Jim!"

"Be still!" said Silver sternly. And Clonmel was silent.

Silver said: "I'll count to three. You shoot then. If either of you stirs a hand before I get to three, I'll shoot that man down—even if it's you, Taxi."

"I understand," said Taxi. "I won't beat the gun."

"I understand," said Christian.

Why, he was smiling now, his head thrown back in the same proud way, and a gleam was in his eyes.

Taxi looked very small, in comparison, but he was a fine mechanism, I knew, with a hand swifter than a cat's paw. He leaned forward a little, staring, intent, savage. After all, he had hated Christian almost as long as Silver had hunted the criminal.

Silver went to Taxi and shook his hand. They said nothing. After all, what could words express between two such men? Then Silver stepped back and began counting.

"One—two—"

I waited through a horrible moment for the count of three. Suddenly I realized that it would never be reached, as Silver, with a groan, exclaimed: "It can't go through! He'll only kill you, Taxi. He's a surer man with a gun!"

"He's not!" said Taxi. "I'll take him with a revolver, or a knife, or a club, or whatever—"

As though he realized his own absurdity, and that his hate was speaking more than his good sense, he stopped himself quickly.

"Get your guns again," said Silver huskily. "It's got to be the law, after all."

"You've had him in prison before, and he's slipped out!" said Taxi. "If you turn him over to the law again, he'll beat you once more. He has the cash to hire lawyers. He has friends to help him escape, if he's headed for the death house. What's the good of going through a game of blindman's bluff again? You have him now! It's the time you've prayed for. Now use it the way he'd use it, if he had the chance."

Silver stood silent, and it was Christian who, with amazing effrontery, said:

"You don't know the honorable gentleman, Taxi."

"Blast you!" breathed Silver, seething with anger.

He went to Christian and jerked the gun from his hand. He tied Christian's wrists behind his back again.

"Go to the edge of the trees and get Parade for me," he directed. "You can tell them to bring Parade to you. The fools will do what you tell them to do."

"Certainly," said Christian. "Any little thing to oblige you, Jim."

We all walked back with Christian and Silver, across the hill, the gully, and over the knoll to the trees around the house. We passed through those, very softly and secretly, and when we were in view of the lighted corral of Parade, Christian stepped out in front of the trees, a pace or two.

"Hello, boys," he said. "I'll show you a trick with Parade. Take the hobbles off him."

"Hello, Barry," said one of the Carys. "What you want us to do that for?"

"I'm going to show you that I've made the big brute into a pet," said Christian. "Take the hobbles off him and you'll see him come to me like a dog."

It was Dean Cary who got through the fence and removed the hobbles.

"You're drunk or you're just talkin', brother," he declared. "Let's see you do your stuff, then!"

Christian nodded, but it was Silver who whistled softly.

The answer was a thing to do your heart good. Parade, when he heard the signal, whirled about and charged the fence as though he were starting a race over the flat. I think the top bar must have been over six feet high, but the big golden monster flew the barrier as though it had been merely knee-high. He made everything look small. He made the mountains and the whole world seem worthless as he flew the fence and, landing in his stride, streaked on toward his master.

"There—you see?" called Christian, stepping back to us, into the shadow of the trees.

Parade went into the group of us, braced his legs to skid to a halt, and tossed his head with a ringing neigh above Silver.

"If you can do that, you can ride him bareback!" called Dean Cary. "Let's see you handle him without a bridle, the way Silver can!"

"I'll be back later, boys," said Christian. "I'm taking a little night trip to get sleepy, just now."

There was an ironic truth in those words of his!

We went back through the trees, Clonmel taking Christian in charge, and Silver leading the way. Then we headed across the Cary Valley towards the biggest gap among the hills, that gap through which I had come and found myself in the beginning of trouble.

26 / At Blue Water

WE WALKED ALL NIGHT LONG. Part of the time Silver made Parade carry Julie Perigord. But after a time, Clonmel began to give out. He had lost a good deal of blood and he had been badly exposed until we wrapped him up in our coats. He swore that he would walk with the rest of us, but Silver and Julie persuaded him to get on the horse, and he was reeling on the back of Parade when at last we got into Blue Water in the pink of the morning.

We made a queer spectacle, I can tell you, as we marched down the main street of that old town. Everybody turned out. It was so early that we might have gone through without attracting much attention, but a small boy got a glimpse of the famous stallion and then spotted Silver. He scampered ahead of us down the street, warning everyone with a voice like the crowning of a rooster.

And all of Blue Water, half dressed, came flooding out around us.

In the middle of all that tumult and cheering—I thought the people would go mad when they saw that Barry Christian was with us—I didn't feel in the least like a hero, because I realized that all I had done was to make Silver's work more difficult.

We got to the jail, and there Silver was met by none other than Sheriff Walt Milton. He hardly had a word for Silver. All he did was to stare at Clonmel.

"You're turning this tramp over to me, too, I guess?" he said. "They want him down in Belling Lake for disturbing the peace and smashing up property."

"Settle the charges out of court, Sheriff," said Silver. "I'll stand for the amount of the damage done."

That ended that discussion. The sheriff looked at Clonmel with hungry eyes, but he had too much sense to go against Silver. What was the use? Judges and juries in our part of the world would never convict a friend of Silver's. He knew that. All he would win would be unpopularity.

So he simply took Christian into the jail.

Christian said good-by to us all in his usual lofty manner. He said, when he looked at me:

"You choose some pretty clumsy weapons now and then, Jim. One of these days, a tool will break and cut your hand for you."

To Silver himself he added directly: "Come see the hanging, Jim, will you?"

Silver said nothing. I think he felt that the hanging would never take place—at least that the law would be much too clumsy to manage the business, even though a capital sentence was already hanging over the head of Christian.

At any rate, we saw the jail doors close between us and the captive.

It was three days later before I drove down into Blue Water again, and got hold of the newspapers that were coming in from the outside, filled with the description of the capture of the famous outlaw.

Even when I read the headlines, I had the feeling

again that Barry Christian was still a long way from being hanged.

That day I had come down with my wife. It was a great trip, in a way. Charlotte had dressed herself all up, and her face was red and a little puffy. And her eyes looked small and bright, and they went quickly from side to side to find and pick up the recognition that people had for us. Because, you see, I was recognized as one of Silver's men, and Jim Silver himself had said a lot about me. Not that there was much to say, but he was the sort of a fellow who knew how to step into the background and put his friends forward, God bless him.

It meant a good deal to me, frankly, but it was plain heaven to Charlotte. A peerage wouldn't have meant any more to her, I guess.

I remember that one of the horses in my team was the mustang that had been under my saddle when I started off that day after Clonmel and Julie. It had simply appeared tied to the hitching rack in front of my house, the morning before!

And now, what did we have on the Cary outfit?

Well, we had the wounds and the sufferings of Clonmel, and the trouble I had been through. But it's hard to collect on threats. I was glad not to push any charge because I didn't want to have the Cary devils on my trail with a grudge. And as for Clonmel, I think he'd almost forgotten that there was such a name as Cary in the world, because he and Julie were getting married this day.

He was in the seventh heaven of happiness. He poured himself out to me when I went to see him at the hotel. He was going to take Julie back East with him, to his parents, and he was going to have Jim in the party. His father and old mother were going to gladden their eyes with the sight of Jim Silver, at last—and that was enough for them. They'd die happy, after that!

Somehow, I felt a doubt. I mean, the idea of Jim Silver in any other setting than the mountains of the West was an anomaly.

But I waited with Charlotte down in the lobby of the hotel, with Charlotte smiling on the reporters who came up to pester us, and with me frowning and scowling at them.

I was feeling stiff in my Sunday clothes, and hot, and uncomfortable, when we started off towards the church behind Clonmel and Julie, and the whole town following us, and cheering like fools. Taxi and Jim Silver were to meet us at the church itself.

And when we got there, the parson was all ready with a welcome—and with a note from Jim Silver! For neither Jim nor Taxi was in sight.

Clonmel read the note, crumpled it, jerked it open, and read it again, with a sick face. Then he passed it over to me, and I read:

DEAR OLD HARRY: Terribly sorry—sudden word has just come, and I have to hop. Will try to be back by tonight to see you and Julie. Luck and happiness to you both.

JIM.

I looked away from the letter to the rolling seas of mountains that turned from green to brown to horizon blue, and I knew very well that that night would not bring Jim Silver back. The wilderness had stretched out its arms to him again, and he was gone far into it.